Rebecca Winters, whose family of four children has now swelled to include five beautiful grandchildren, lives in Salt Lake City, Utah, in the land of the Rocky Mountains. Living near canyons and high alpine meadows full of wildflowers, she never runs out of places to explore. They, plus her favorite vacation spots in Europe, often end up as backgrounds for her romance novels, because writing is her passion, along with her family and church.

Rebecca loves to hear from readers. If you wish to email her, please visit her website, cleanromances.net.

The Right Cowboy

REBECCA WINTERS

MILLS & BOON

First published in Great Britain 2018
by Mills & Boon, an imprint of HarperCollins*Publishers*
1 London Bridge Street, London, SE1 9GF

Large Print edition 2018

© 2018 Rebecca Winters

ISBN: 978-0-263-07775-9

MIX
Paper from
responsible sources
FSC C007454

This book is produced from independently certified
FSC™ paper to ensure responsible forest management.
For more information visit www.harpercollins.co.uk/green.

Printed and bound in Great Britain
by CPI Group (UK) Ltd, Croydon, CR0 4YY

To my darling hairdresser Alicia, who has become a friend and has kept me looking great. (Great as *I* can look.) The poor thing has had to listen to some of my stories—which she has done with patience—even though she just wanted a simple sentence or two of explanation. *Never ask a writer what she's been working on!* If you want to hear some of her brother's terrific country-and-western music, check out his website: jaredrogerson.com.

Chapter One

Tamsin Rayburn pulled in her parking space in front of Ostler Certified Accounting Firm in Whitebark, Wyoming. She was running late to get back to the ranch. Dean would be picking her up for dinner and she needed to hurry.

With her light chestnut hair swishing against her shoulders, she got out of the car and rushed through the reception area to her office. Her boss would be pleased to know she'd finished auditing the books for Beckstrand Drilling earlier than planned and could start on the Whitebark Hospital audit.

In her haste, she almost ran into Heather Jennings, a coworker who'd become a close friend over the last two years. It looked like everyone else had gone home. Smiling at her she said, "I've never needed a weekend more. How about you?"

Heather studied her for a moment with an anxious expression. "You don't know, do you?"

She was being very mysterious. "Know what?"

"I've been hoping you would walk in here before I left. Now I'm almost afraid to tell you."

"Heather—what's wrong?"

Her friend drew in a deep breath. "There's only one way to say this. Today I had lunch with Amy Paskett." Amy was a girl Tamsin had known from high school who worked at Paskett's feed store. "It turns out her father waited on Cole Hawkins this morning. Apparently he's back in Whitebark for good."

Tamsin grabbed the edge of her desk while her world whirled for a moment. "Wh-what did you say?" she stammered.

"I knew this would be hard for you to hear."

Cole was home for good? The cowboy who'd left the state nine years ago, riding off with her heart?

The last time she'd seen him was at a distance when he'd come home for his father's funeral six months ago. He'd been driving down the street in a friend's truck, but he hadn't seen her. Once the funeral was over, he'd left again.

Shock didn't begin to describe what she was feeling. "How long has he been here?"

"I don't know. That was all Amy said in passing. I've been waiting to tell you in case you hadn't heard. If you hadn't come, I would have phoned you."

Tamsin looked at Heather, still reeling from the incredible news. "Thank you for being such a good friend." Heather knew some of her past history with Cole, but not all.

"I'm not sure *thanks* is the right word."

"Yes, it is." She gave her a hug. "I'm grateful to have heard it from you first. Now at least I'm prepared should someone else tell me."

"Look—I've got to go, but call me this weekend and we'll talk."

She nodded. "I'll walk out with you."

Tamsin waited while Heather locked up, then she hurried to her car. She was so shaken by what her friend had told her, she trembled all the way to her family's ranch located two miles south of town.

There'd been an article in the *Sublette Gazette* four months ago about the rodeo legend Cole Hawkins being involved with a country singer from Colorado. It didn't surprise Tamsin since he was a talented musician and songwriter himself. Maybe he'd married the woman and had brought her home to settle down.

If he were recently married, how would Tamsin be able to handle it, knowing she'd be seeing them coming and going?

After he'd left Wyoming, she'd worked through her sorrow day and night for several years to earn enough money to put herself through college. Once she'd finished her schooling, she'd spent the last four years throwing herself into her career as a CPA.

At twenty-seven she had dreams of opening up her own agency one day, and she'd been dating Dean Witcom, an amazing man.

Their relationship had grown serious. Lately she was excited about where it was headed. He'd be a wonderful, devoted husband just like his brother Lyle who adored her sister.

Yet the mere mention of Cole—let alone that he was home to stay—sent stabbing pain through her as if it were only yesterday he'd said goodbye to her. She couldn't bear it, not when she'd fought with everything in her power to put his memory behind her. If her sister Sally knew about Cole, she'd kept quiet about it.

Once Tamsin reached the ranch house, she felt a guilty pang when she saw that Dean's truck with the Witcom-Dennison Oil Association logo was parked out in front. How could she be thinking about Cole when Dean was here waiting for her? What was wrong with her?

She drove around the back and rushed inside to find her sister. Sally and her husband, Lyle, who also worked at WDOA, were living temporarily at the ranch. They were probably in the living room talking to Dean while he passed the time until Tamsin got home. No one else was in the house. Their parents were on a vacation in Afton to visit extended family.

Dean had told her to get dressed up. Tamsin had the suspicion he'd planned something special. She'd been looking forward to it and had bought a new dress, but there was no way she could enjoy an evening with him tonight and pretend nothing was wrong.

"Sally?" She knocked on their bedroom door in case she was in there. The family's golden retriever came running up to lick her. "Hey, Duke. Is Sally in there?" She rubbed the dog's head.

Her pregnant younger sister opened the door,

finishing pulling a loose-fitting top over her maternity jeans. "Tamsin—" She looked surprised to see her.

"I'm so glad you were in here." Sally was the one person who knew everything about her heartbreak over Cole and had consoled her through the worst of those early days when she'd thought her life had ended.

"What's wrong? You look like you've seen a ghost."

"Not a ghost." She hugged her arms to her waist. "Cole's back."

Her sister's eyes—sky blue like Tamsin's—narrowed in disbelief. "Come on in."

Tamsin stepped past her. Duke rushed in before Sally shut the door behind her. "You actually saw him?" The question revealed that her sister hadn't known anything, either.

"I just came from work. Heather told me

he'd been seen at Paskett's feed store this morning. Do you think Lyle knows?"

"No. Otherwise he would have told me and I would have phoned you." She put a hand on Tamsin's arm. "Did you know Dean is here? Lyle's out in the front room with him."

Tamsin nodded. "I saw his truck, but I need time to recover from the shock. Ever since I started seeing your brother-in-law four months ago, I assured him there'd been no other man in my life for a long time. At this point I'm totally involved with him, but Dean's not going to trust me if he finds out the real reason why I'm so upset tonight. I can't believe how this news has affected me."

"I can. Let's face it. You never got over him."

"Yes, I did!" she defended.

"Then why has this news caused you to lose all the color in your face?"

She lowered her head. "You're exaggerating."

"Look in the mirror."

"I'm going to be fine."

"I hope that's true. As far as I'm concerned, Cole Hawkins made the biggest mistake of his life by walking away from you. He was a fool and *never* deserved you. What astounds me is that he still has the power to do this to you after being gone for so long. Don't let him do this to you." Her voice shook.

"You think I want to feel like this? Oh, Sally. What am I going to do? I guess this day had to come and I've made too much over it be-cause—because I always wondered what it would be like to see him again. I just need to-night to put everything into perspective. Can you understand?"

"Of course I do."

"Dean's the man I care about now."

"I know, and he's so crazy about you it's sickening."

"Thanks."

"You know what I mean. Look. Stay in here. I'll go out and tell Dean you've come home with a migraine and will call him later."

"I hate doing this to him, but there's no way I can hide my reaction right now. I'm afraid it will show and ruin the evening he has planned. I'll have to sleep on it. In the morning, everything will be all right. I'll phone him and let him know I'm so sorry."

"Don't worry. I'll be convincing."

Tamsin hugged her sister who was only two years younger. Some people actually thought they were twins. "Thanks, Sally. What would I do without you?"

"I say that about you all the time. If you hadn't been there championing me during my barrel racing days when I couldn't get it together, I don't know how I would have made

it. I'll be back in a minute and we'll talk."
Duke followed her out the door.

COLE HAWKINS HAD only been asleep five
hours Sunday night when the pager on the
side table went off at ten after three in the
morning. He shot out of bed and put on jeans
and a T-shirt. After grabbing his keys, he hurried to the back porch of the ranch house to
pull on his turnout gear. His Ford-350 diesel
truck was parked nearby for a quick exit in
the warm late-June air.

He climbed inside and headed for the fire
station in Whitebark, three miles away. The
small town of thirteen hundred people was
nestled at the base of the Wind River Range of
the Rocky Mountains, known as "The Winds"
by those who'd been born and raised there
like Cole.

Located in the west-central part of the state,

the crest of the magnificent range silhouetted under tonight's half-moon ran along the Continental Divide. Gannett Peak rose 13,804 feet, the highest in Wyoming. That image of home had been inscribed in Cole's mind and heart forever, having grounded him during his nine years away.

During the time he'd been at the University of Colorado in Boulder to complete undergraduate and graduate school, he'd also managed to become a firefighter. After working his tail off, he was finally back in Whitebark, ready to get started on his career, *and* do something drastic about his aching heart.

There was only one woman in this world who could fix it. He knew Tamsin didn't want to see him…not ever. But that was too damn bad because when he'd come home for his father's funeral six months ago, he'd heard she wasn't married yet. Now that he was back in

Wyoming territory, he planned to stake his claim no matter how long it took.

More determined than he'd ever been in his life, Cole roared into town and drove around the back of the station to park. Grabbing his helmet, he ran through to the bay and climbed in the tender truck.

Wyatt Fielding, an old friend who'd done bull riding with him in high school, was driving. They took off with the blare of the siren and lights flashing. This baby held twenty-five hundred gallons of water; an accident could be disastrous. He grinned at Cole.

"It's so great to have you back after all this time. I couldn't believe it the other day when Chief Powell told us you'd signed on with the department here."

"Only when I'm available. There'll be times when I'm up in the mountains working."

"Understood. I guess you realize you're still a rodeo legend around these parts."

"So were you."

"That's bull and you know it. I was never good enough to go on the circuit."

"Well, those days are over for me, Wyatt. I'm just thankful to be home at last."

"You and I have a lot of catching up to do, but we'll have to do it later. A fire has broken out on the Circle R Ranch. The ladder truck already took off. Captain Durrant is waiting for us."

Circle R... "You don't mean Rayburn's—"

"There's only one Rayburn in Whitebark."

Cole's heart started to thud unmercifully. Tamsin Rayburn, the girl he'd come home for, *if* she was still living there. A fire had broken out on *her* family's ranch? He couldn't believe it. Maybe he was going to see her sooner than he'd planned, but fear seized him that she could be in danger.

While Wyatt took the turnoff for the ranch, Cole's mind relived their history that went back to his senior year in high school when they'd fallen madly in love. But circumstances beyond his control had separated them. She'd stopped returning his letters and phone calls. She'd even changed her phone number.

When he did visit his father periodically during those years, he knew she wanted nothing to do with him. Until he was home for good, he couldn't do anything about their situation.

Cole had only been back in Wyoming five days. His first responsibility lay with his family's longtime friend and foreman, Sam Speakuna, and his wife, Louise. They were Arapahoes from the Northern Arapahoe reservation who'd come to work for his father early on. Over the years they'd spent part of the time in their apartment on the Hawkins' ranch, and commuted to Lander where they had a home and could be with their family.

All the time Cole had been away, those two had shouldered the full responsibility of the ranch house and the crew of two wranglers who handled their herd of forty head of beef cattle. They were like family to him at this point. Now it was time to discuss their future and the future of the Hawkins' small cattle ranch.

After a meeting with Fire Chief Owen Powell, who'd received Cole's credentials from Colorado, he took him on board immediately. After his father's funeral, Cole had talked to Chief Powell about the possibility of his coming on board when his time in Colorado was over.

The chief was overjoyed at the prospect, telling him Whitebark could never have enough firefighters. Cole knew that was true. It helped to know he would have a place in the department. It wasn't just the extra income, but that sense of belonging he needed to feel after being away so long.

His own father had combined firefighting and ranching. Now that Cole was back, he'd honored his father's wishes to follow in his footsteps and do his part for the community, too. But he'd hardly had a chance to catch his breath before the pager had awakened him tonight.

The Circle R lay outside Whitebark at the other end of town. Cole had been there many times before in the past saying good-night to Tamsin. He could have found it blindfolded. Tonight he could see flames shooting up in the sky from the barn before they even drove in.

When they arrived, Cole heard quiet pandemonium and horses squealing. A mob of ranch hands had assembled. They were rescuing the animals and leading them toward the paddock in the distance. His eyes searched frantically for Tamsin but saw no sign of her or her parents. Maybe she wasn't even here.

While the guys on the ladder truck were working the hoses, the captain signaled Wyatt to go to the other end of the barn. As they drove around, Cole whistled. "Somebody left an old wooden work ladder against that window. My gut tells me an arsonist has been at work."

"I think you're right."

The second Wyatt parked the truck, they both jumped out and started pumping water. Their job was to put out any new spots of flames shooting up through the boards. Black smoke was curling out from the seams.

After a few minutes, everything looked under control from their side. They turned off the pump and racked the hoses before driving around to the front of the barn. A couple of the crew were inside looking for hot spots.

Captain Durrant worked as incident commander. He and another fire department official walked over to him and Wyatt. "It's good to have you aboard, Cole."

"I'm glad to be here, sir."

"Call me Jeff. This is Commissioner Rich, head of the arson squad."

The older man nodded to Cole. "Did you see anything that caught your attention around the other side?"

"There's an old work ladder propped by the window. We figured the arsonist used it to either get in, or climb up on the roof and make a hole to whip up the speed and intensity of blaze. Evidently he didn't have time to hide it."

"Good." The commissioner eyed Wyatt. "Do you have anything else to add?"

"Yes. The black smoke indicates an accelerant was used. I couldn't smell it around the side, but I can smell gasoline fumes here." The barn had become an unusable disaster.

"There's been a series of ranch fires that have broken out in Sublette County over the last three months," the older man informed them. "Not all have been the same and we haven't been able to solve the logic of them yet, but every bit of information helps. Thanks for the creditable information. It ties in with the forensics evidence on these other cases that an accelerant was used."

After he walked away to do his own inspection, Cole turned to the captain. "I used to know the people who live here. Where are they?"

"Howard Rayburn and his wife are out of town. Apparently their dog started barking and woke up the other members of the family. They're probably with the horses. I believe their son-in-law, Lyle Witcom, called 911."

Cole reeled. "Did you say son-in-law?"

"Yes. He's married to one of their daughters."

Maybe his information about Tamsin had been wrong. Please God, let it be her younger sister, Sally. The very thought of it being the woman who'd always had a stranglehold on his heart shook him to the core of his being.

Before he lost his grip, he said, "Their horses are going to need a new home until this barn is rebuilt. The barn on my ranch has room for six more horses. I could drive home and bring my rig to transport them."

"I have no idea what arrangements they plan to make, but I'll let them know of your generous offer."

Before Cole could say anything else, another member of the crew called to Jeff, diverting his attention. Cole turned to Wyatt. "While we walk around the barn again to find more hot spots, tell me which Rayburn sister is married. Do you know?"

Wyatt eyed him curiously. "It's Sally. She married Lyle Witcom last year."

With that news Cole was able to breathe again. Everything about this unexpected night had him so tied up in knots he was losing his concentration.

They started another inspection. After twenty minutes they finished examining the exterior of the barn, looking for any evidence that could help identify the arsonist.

"If this guy loves to set fires to watch things burn up for the hell of it, he got careless here."

"Something must have frightened him off," Cole murmured. "If there've been a lot of fires lately, I'm thinking this freak has a definite agenda and that means he needs help to coordinate these raids. I'd be willing to bet he's doing this with a bunch of guys out for some kind of revenge."

Wyatt flashed him a glance. "For what reason?"

"Fire bugs don't need much to go on a rampage. I saw it over in Colorado. The motive in that case had to do with a group trying to intimidate a legislator on the marijuana issue. They were caught and brought up on criminal charges, but not before a lot of damage was done to his property and he spent time in the hospital."

"Incredible." They waved to the guys on the ladder truck who were cleaning up. "Shall we go back to the station?"

"Give me a minute, Wyatt. I'll be right back."

Cole broke into a run as he headed for the corral where he could see some hands gentling the horses. A little closer now, he glimpsed the woman he'd been searching for rubbing her horse's forelock. Her back was toward him. The ponytail looked painfully familiar.

The blood pounded in his ears. "Tamsin?" he called to her.

She turned around, causing his second shock for the night because it was her sister in the last stages of pregnancy who faced him, not Tamsin.

The last time Cole had seen Sally, she'd been sixteen and had just ridden in the local teen rodeo. But her disappointing marks had devastated her and she'd cried against Tamsin's shoulder. Both sisters bore a strong resemblance to each other and had been touchingly devoted.

"Do I know you?"

Whoa. With his five-o'clock shadow and helmet, she obviously didn't recognize him. Or maybe she did and pretended not to. Probably the latter since he knew she had no love for him. He removed his helmet.

Her features tightened as she studied him. "So the rumors really are true. The great rodeo legend who rode off chasing his dreams is back and working as a firefighter, no less. Who would have thought? If you turn your head, you'll see my sister—she's right over there." Her eyes narrowed. "You just can't help yourself, can you? But if you approach her, you do it at your own peril."

Sally turned back to her horse.

A kick in the gut from a wild mustang couldn't have been more debilitating than her warning. But he shouldn't really be surprised when he knew the girls had been each other's best friend all their lives.

Without saying another word, he looked around and saw Tamsin talking to one of the stockmen while she patted her horse's neck.

He walked closer to her, holding the helmet under his arm.

The unremarkable jeans and T-shirt she must have put on when the alarm sounded only emphasized the gorgeous mold of her body and long legs.

First light had already crept across the sky. That pink tone added a tint to her skin and highlighted the shape of the delectable mouth he'd dreamed of kissing and tasting every night.

Her hair hung to her shoulders. He picked out the streaks of gold among the light chestnut sheen no artificial color could improve upon. Once again her natural beauty took his breath.

Maybe she heard his quickly indrawn breath because her eyes suddenly swerved to his. Though she made no motion of any kind, he could sense the stiffening of her body.

"I'm sorry about the fire, Tamsin, but I'm happy to see all your horses are safe. If you need a place to stall them for a while, I have space in my barn and will transport them for you. I've already informed the captain. All you have to do is say the word and I'll be back to load them within the hour."

"Thank you," she said through wooden lips. "We've already had three offers and my brother-in-law is taking care of the arrangements as we speak."

"Tamsin—" He said her name again, but by now another man with brown hair wearing chinos and a polo shirt had come running into the corral and threw possessive arms around her as if she belonged to him. Cole watched her melt against his body. She'd obviously done it before and buried her face against his shoulder.

If this was the kind of peril Sally had been

talking about, then Cole got the point. It was more like he'd been run through by Tamsin's twelve-foot lance on the field of battle. He turned away and walked back to the burned barn where Wyatt was waiting for him.

The ladder truck had already started back to town. Cole climbed in the tender truck and they took off. His body felt like it weighed a thousand pounds.

Wyatt flashed him a side glance. "Are you all right?"

"I don't know. Ask me in the morning."

"It already is morning."

So it was.

"Do you want to stop for coffee and doughnuts at Hilda's?"

No, but he knew Wyatt wanted to. "Sure. I could use both. Does this mean you don't have a wife at home who will fix your breakfast when you get there?"

"What woman would that be?"

Cole actually chuckled. "Amen to that. You've just described my life, Wyatt. A half hour ago I was warned that if I approached the woman I was looking for, I had to do it at my own peril. That turned out to be true, unfortunately."

"You're talking about Tamsin. I remember back in high school when you two were so close during our senior year, I couldn't imagine that changing."

"At the time, I couldn't, either. Now we live in separate universes."

"So *that's* why you came back to the truck looking like one of the walking dead."

"Thanks."

"Hey—have you taken a good look at me? We could be brothers. Welcome to the club. We're great at wrangling steers, herding sheep or fighting fires. Give us any task, but get us around a woman and we just don't know how to do it right."

"You said a mouthful."

"I don't mean you, specifically, Cole. I've been a mess for a long time and I don't see that changing anytime soon. There are more guys like us in the department. Take Porter Ewing, who's a recent transfer with the forest service from New York. He swings in when needed. The dude's convinced there's no woman alive who would want him."

Cole laughed out loud despite the pain of seeing Tamsin in that other guy's arms. He'd always liked Wyatt. His sense of humor was a welcome balm to the horrific experience he'd just lived through. Only one thing saved him from oblivion. She wasn't married yet.

Welcome home, Cole.

Chapter Two

While some of the hands stayed with the horses in the paddock, Dean walked Tamsin back to the house with his arm around her shoulders. "Thank God none of you were hurt. When Lyle phoned me, I was terrified that the ranch house might have caught fire, too."

"But it didn't, and I'm fine." She appreciated his trying to comfort her over the loss of the barn. Naturally she was thankful they'd gotten the horses out in time. But he had no clue what a traumatic night this had turned out to be when she saw all six foot two of Cole Hawkins walk toward her.

He was a firefighter? She was incredulous.

Was he out of his mind after the horrific fire in the Winds nine years ago?

Her best friend Mandy had lost her father in that fire. Tamsin had loved her dad. She and Cole had gone to his funeral. Everyone was grief-stricken over the loss. Eleven other firefighters from their county alone had been trapped and killed in the blaze that had brought other firefighters from around the country to fight it.

Maybe she'd been hallucinating.

But no… When she'd opened her eyes again, there he'd been. In cowboy hat and boots or firefighter gear, no man could touch his dark blond masculine beauty. He was an outstanding athlete with a rock-hard body that made him a breed apart. Over the years that he'd been gone and all the dates with other guys, his image had always gotten in the way. Damn, *damn* him.

For him to have stood there now with a quiet authority while he offered his barn for their horses—the first words she'd heard him speak in years, as if there'd been no separation or pain—she'd surprised herself that she could respond to him at all. When Dean came running up to her, she'd clung to him because she'd thought she was going to faint. Thank Heaven he'd attributed her state of mind to the fire while she watched Cole walk away on his powerful legs.

Of course it had been frightening to see flames shooting up from the barn, but they'd soon gotten the horses out and the firefighters had come. The shudders she was experiencing now had their roots in coming face-to-face with Cole, knowing he made his living by walking into danger.

The teenage guy she'd fallen crazy in love with existed no more. In nine years he'd turned into a breathtaking man who'd come home a firefighter. She couldn't comprehend this new image of him. It meant his life could be snuffed out at any moment.

When she and Dean walked in the kitchen, they heard Lyle on the phone making final arrangements for the horses. He'd fixed coffee for them, but one look at Sally's drawn pale face while she drank some bottled water worried Tamsin. Duke stood guard.

"Excuse me for a minute, Dean." She eased herself away from him and put a hand on her sister's shoulder. "Come on, Sally. You need to get back to bed. There's been too much excitement and I'm sure it has raised your blood pressure."

"Okay."

At Sally's six-month checkup, the doctor had said he wanted her to lie down part of every day until she delivered. At that point, their mom had asked her and Lyle to stay at the ranch until the baby was born, where she could be waited on while Lyle was at work. So Sally and Lyle had given up their apartment in town, with plans to move into another one after the baby was born.

Tamsin walked Sally to their bedroom and Duke followed. She waited for her to emerge from the bathroom in her nightgown. Once she got in bed, Tamsin sat down next to her. Duke plopped down at her feet.

"How are you feeling? I have half a mind to call Dr. Ward."

"No, don't do that. I'm fine now. Duke woke us all up in time. He's a hero."

Tamsin smiled down at the dog. "He sure

is. I almost had a heart attack when I looked out the window and saw the flames. It sounds like Roy next door will be letting us board our horses at his place until we get the barn rebuilt. We're so lucky."

Her sister stared at her with unswerving intensity. "I agree, but I'm afraid *you're* the one I'm worried about now. You're so pale."

She couldn't pretend with Sally. "I admit I've been a mess since I heard the news Cole was back. But seeing him tonight in firefighter gear gave me another shock."

"Don't you mean seeing him in the *flesh*? That expression took on new meaning for me tonight, too. He's really something. Did I ever tell you I used to have a crush on him?"

Tamsin smiled without mirth. "You and everyone else. What helps me is knowing that he's either married or getting close to marrying that singer I read about in the *Sublette Gazette* a few months ago."

"I saw him talk to you. What did he say?"

She sucked in her breath. "As calm as a hot summer day, he said he'd be happy to board our horses. He even offered to bring his rig over and load them."

Sally gripped her hand. "What did you say back?"

"Don't worry, sister dear. I learned my lesson a long time ago. As Dean was coming toward me, I told Cole that arrangements had already been made. You have no idea the joy I felt to shove the offer in that good-looking face of his before he walked away."

Her sister took another drink of water. "I don't get it. I thought he rode the circuit to make money because he was the hotshot bull rider and wanted the fame. All that pain he caused you when he could have stayed right here and become a firefighter… What was the point?"

"To get away from me, of course," Tamsin murmured. Nothing else made sense. The circuit meant being surrounded by women who would idolize him. Why would he stay in Whitebark? Tamsin had been such a fool, and what a consummate liar he'd turned out to be!

The letters she'd stopped reading and the phone messages she wouldn't listen to were tokens of his supposed guilt. What a joke! It sickened her. Sally spoke the truth. He could have stayed here to become a firefighter. But no. He had to strive for fame and glory. She'd never have thought he was that type of man back when they were dating.

"I don't want to talk about him. Married to some singing celebrity or not, free to do whatever he wants, he's been out of my life for nine years. Compared to Dean..." She shook her head. "I've got my own life to think about, and I'm furious I've spent one more minute thinking about him. You know?"

"I believe you."

Tamsin smiled sadly at her sister. "No, you don't, but I'm going to prove you wrong."

"Where are you going?"

"To talk to Dean. Try to get some more sleep, Sally. I'll see you later."

"Okay."

Duke stayed by her sister while Tamsin walked through to the kitchen. "Your wife is comfortable now, Lyle. She's going to catch up on some sleep."

"Good." He looked relieved and had made breakfast. She joined them at the table. "Dean's going to help me load the horses to take over to the Ingram ranch."

"I'm going to help you, too. It'll go a lot faster. Did you phone Dad?"

He nodded. "Sally and I did it together earlier. They're coming home today. We talked about whom to hire to start rebuilding the barn."

"How upset was he?"

"Your father believes it's someone working for the forest service who has a grudge against the government and some of their policies. Your dad has seen this behavior before. A few crazies out there try to take the law into their own hands and start fires. In your father's case, they want him to stop allowing his cattle to graze on forest land even though he has the legal right."

"That's horrible." She looked at Dean. "Do you think Dad's insurance will cover the arson damage completely?"

"I'd have to take a look at the policy."

"When the police catch the man who did this, I hope he goes to prison for the rest of his life!"

On that note, they finished eating. Lyle got up from the table first. "While I go in and check on Sally, will you find the keys to the horse trailer rig? Then we'll start loading the horses."

Tamsin nodded. "They're in Dad's study. I'll get them. Be right back." She hurried through the house and got the keys out of his desk. When she returned to the kitchen, Dean was loading the dishwasher.

"You don't need to be washing our dishes."

He turned his attractive head in her direction. "What if I want to?"

Dean was that kind of guy and so rock solid. She could never find a better man who would always be there for her. Loving him for those qualities, she walked over and gave him a hug.

"You've done enough. Let's go load the horses."

He kissed her thoroughly before they left the house. For the last month he'd wanted to take their relationship to a more intimate level. Tamsin had held back, but for the life of her she couldn't understand why. He was a terrific man and had been so understanding the other night about breaking their date.

Because he and Lyle were brothers, he was over at the ranch a lot. The cozy situation threw the four of them together all the time. She and Dean didn't have enough privacy. Maybe that needed to change. Not for the first time had she thought about getting her own apartment.

What was she waiting for? Seeing Cole again made her realize she'd been living in a deep freeze while he was out having the time of his life. It was time to do something about it.

The more she thought about it, the more she realized she needed her independence. It was long past time Tamsin lived on her own. She'd stayed around her family too long. They'd been there for her after Cole had ridden out of her life, helping her to recover. And she'd gone along allowing it to continue.

She'd saved enough money to get a place of her own. With the horses having to be boarded for at least a couple of months away from the ranch, now would be the time to leave. Her family could wait on Sally.

Once Tamsin was on her own, maybe she would discover just how in love she was with Dean. It was time to find out. After seeing Cole again, all she knew was that she needed perspective to get her head on straight. His arrival in town seemed to have served as a wakeup call, pulling her out of a deep sleep.

All this and more ran through her head while she and Dean helped Lyle load the horses from the paddock and drive them to their new temporary location. Before the day was over, she planned to get online and see what housing rentals were available. The sooner the better.

Two hours later, they'd accomplished their objective. Tamsin did everything in her power to make the horses comfortable in their temporary home, especially her mare Flossie. While she fed her some treats, Dean put his arm around her shoulders.

"You love her the way some people love their children."

She chuckled. "I guess I do."

He turned her around. "Last night I almost lost it when I thought you might have been hurt in that fire. It's all I've been able to think about." With that admission he gave her another long kiss she welcomed.

"I was so thankful you came over when you did!"

"I never want to be separated from you. I wish I didn't have to leave now, but I have an important meeting at work. I'll call you later and we'll get together tonight."

"I'd like that." She meant it. Cole had come home and she'd survived seeing him again. But it was Dean she cared about now and she wanted to show him.

AT EIGHT O'CLOCK Tuesday morning Cole walked into the fire station wearing jeans and one of his long-sleeved denim shirts. He'd been getting ready to go to work on his new job when Chief Powell summoned him to attend an emergency meeting.

When he entered the conference room, he

saw a large group of firefighters assembled plus Chief Powell and Commissioner Rich, head of the arson unit. Other men had been called in, too, several of whom wore police uniforms.

Wyatt sat in one corner and signaled to Cole, who joined him in the empty seat next to him. "What's going on with the big confab?"

"I guess we're going to find out."

Another couple of guys walked in the room and found a seat before Chief Powell got to his feet. "Gentlemen? Thanks for coming on such short notice. We've had a serious arson problem here in Sublette County for the past three months. Commissioner Rich, the head of the Arson Task Force, has called a meeting of all of us for help. As I read your names, will you please stand?

"Whitebark Police Chief Holden Granger—

"Director Arnie Blunt of the Wyoming State Fire Services Department—

"Norm Selkirk, head of Sublette County Law Enforcement—

"Orson Perone, regional head of Wyoming forestry that includes fire prevention—

"Thank you, gentlemen. Now I'd like to turn over the meeting to Commissioner Rich."

The sixtyish-looking, sandy-haired man got to his feet. "I've been interviewing the owners of the other ranches who've been hit with fires in the last three months. I've just come from interviewing the owner of the Circle R Ranch, Howard Rayburn, the latest victim in this rash of fires. It happened just two days ago.

"He wasn't home at the time, but he believes he's being targeted for using forest land to let his cattle graze there despite his legal right. Occasionally someone comes out of the woodwork upset over this practice. He's seen it before."

Cole bowed his head. The memory of those few painful moments with Tamsin in the paddock were still too fresh not to be affected by what he was hearing.

"What I'd like is to get an opinion from each of you, especially the crew from this station who fought the fire the other night. Anything you tell us in this meeting could be valuable no matter how insignificant you think it might be.

"Before I call on you one at a time, I'll pass out a map that shows the location of each fire and read the list I've compiled of what we know about them. In all cases, a ranch was targeted."

Once the maps were distributed, he began talking. While Cole listened, he kept studying the areas of Sublette County where the fires had been set and thought he saw a pattern in their locations. His mind kept harkening back to something his mentor had explained in detail during the last year of his graduate studies.

"They were all started in the middle of the night with no witnesses, and an accelerant was used every time," the commissioner explained.

"Eight fires were set inside the fencing that holds the stacked hay bales. None were locked. No lightning was involved.

"The other two were set inside barns where it was estimated that the large fire load of hay inside the barn must have been burning twenty to thirty minutes before it was detected. The electrical wiring and all other potential accidental causes of the fires have been ruled out and no lightning was involved.

"The public outcry is mandating a response

to solve these crimes despite the availability of only circumstantial evidence. These fires have now become a priority for the criminal justice system. We're preparing a flier to distribute to every rancher in the county. They need to be alerted to the impending danger to their property and figure out ways to safeguard it.

"We're hoping those warnings will make a difference, but we need to pick the brains of you men who fight these fires every day. Your instincts could help to save lives and millions of dollars. Why don't we go around the back row first and get your opinions? Please state your name and tell us how long you've been with the department."

Cole heard a lot of grudge theories, but nothing specific. When it came to his turn, he got to his feet. "I'm Cole Hawkins. I grew up right here in Whitebark and went to college in Boulder, Colorado. While I was studying, I also trained to become a firefighter with the Boulder Fire Department. I planned to come home to the ranch after graduation and combine my work with firefighting the way my dad did."

He looked at the commissioner. "When you were giving the statistics, I was curious to know if this kind of an outbreak with this same set of circumstances is unique to this year only."

The older man shook his head. "We saw this happen last year to six ranches, but this year's number of outbreaks has increased and summer isn't over."

"Were the fires set at the same time of year last year?"

"Come to think of it, yes, around the end of April and running through August."

"If you had a map of last year's locations of fires, where would they be?"

He stared at Cole. "I'm not sure."

Chief Powell broke in. "I'll get on the computer right now and we'll find out." Within minutes he had the answer. "All of them were near the Winds."

Cole got excited. "Then that cycle fits with the fire locations on the map you just handed out to us. Notice that every ranch targeted this year and last is close to the Bridger Wilderness."

At this point he'd caught everyone's attention.

"There's a war going on between the ranchers hunting the elk coming down from the mountain onto their property, and the ranchers who are against elk hunting."

"Go on," the commissioner urged him.

"Years ago, the elk in the snow country

The Right Cowboy

came down to the desert to find food, hay particularly. They ate in the cattle feed grounds where the cattle carried brucellosis disease that caused the cattle to abort. It was transferred to the elk. By the 1930s, calves were dying and humans started getting sick with undulant fever, until pasteurization came along. It's been a battle ever since to eradicate the disease.

"You want a reason for these fires? I believe they've been set to warn the ranchers allowing the hunting. The conservationists want the elk rerouted down to the desert in different migration paths that don't come into contact with the cattle feed lines so the disease won't spread.

"But other ranchers want to bring in the big game hunters who pay a lot of money for the elk hunt. With the hay left out and exposed, the elk are lured to the ranches, thus ensuring plenty of elk for a good hunt. A lot of hay could feed a thousand cattle a day, and the elk, too."

"How do you know so much about this?"

"When I was young, my father used to complain about the brucellosis disease that caused cattle to abort. He hoped that one day it would be eradicated. By the time I went to college, I decided to go into that field and ended up getting my master's to be a brucellosis ecologist.

"I learned that some cattle brought into the States by early European settlers carried this disease. In my role as an ecologist, we're trying to manage the disease and lower it in the elk herds so it's less likely to spill over into cattle."

Orson Perone stood up. "Mr. Hawkins is absolutely right about this. A few years ago there was a small town near the Owl Creek Mountains where the elk had spread disease to a local cattle herd. The fish and game had to depopulate the herd. This caused the ranchers to go bankrupt and the pattern is still the same today. Unfortunately it made for bad relations."

The commissioner looked at Cole. "So it's your contention that there's a group of cattle ranchers sending messages to the ranchers who allow elk hunting to stop luring the elk with hay, and they're resorting to arson to make their point."

Cole nodded. "It makes sense to me considering that all sixteen fires were set in an attempt to destroy the hay as soon as it's harvested."

A collective silence filled the room. The older man smiled at Cole. "Well, aren't we glad you came back home and joined our fire department? I think you're really on to something here."

"I know he is." Holden Granger had gotten to his feet. "I was born and raised in Cody, Wyoming, before I moved here. Our family's ranch suffered a loss of cattle from that disease when I was young. No one ever established a link with the diseased elk that often came to the cattle feed grounds from the Absaroka Mountains."

At this point Chief Powell took over. "Now that we've been educated, we'll explain about the disease in the warning fliers and have them ready by next Monday. By hand or through the mail we'll make certain they're distributed to all the ranchers, urging them to take emergency precautions to ward off the arsonists plaguing parts of Sublette County."

"Excellent," Holden commented. "With this information, I'm going to get together with the county prosecutor. With the cooperation of Norm and Orson, particularly, we can start making lists of ranchers who've never applied for hunting licenses or permits. I'd like to know when and where this group of arsonists meets. That means we'll need a warrant from the judge.

"Setting fires isn't the solution to eradicating the disease. We'll canvas every store that sells accelerants. This is only the beginning." He nodded to Cole. "I'd like to talk to you alone. When you have time, drop by the police station."

"If you want, I'll come now because I'll be leaving for the mountains on my job as soon we're finished and be gone four days."

"Then come with me."

Cole turned to Wyatt. "I'll see you when I get back."

"I plan on it."

Everyone shook Cole's hand before he left with the sheriff. But he was weighed down with worry because Tamsin's father had been targeted and it could happen again before the summer was over. He needed to talk to her and warn her, but he'd have to do that when he got back.

While he was packing his gear to leave for the mountains, he got a text from Patsy Janis.

Call me ASAP. I've got big news.

Cole shook his head. He'd only been home five days and already she couldn't leave him alone. She never gave up. He'd met the good-looking local country singer two years ago in Colorado at a concert in Boulder. He'd grown up on country music, playing the guitar and composing his own songs. Early on he'd made certain to sign up with ASCAP to get his songs copyrighted.

Patsy had a lot of talent and was featured weekends at a local club near the campus with lots of college students and wannabe musicians who got together to jam. It was definitely his kind of place and a great outlet when he'd had a surfeit of studying and needed to get away from it for a little while.

She'd found out he composed music, too, and coaxed him to let her sing some of his songs. Pretty soon, he was accompanying her on his guitar while she sang his tunes for their enthusiastic audience. Everyone wanted to hear more.

Little by little, she encouraged him to do a few recordings at the studio with her just for fun. It wasn't long before they'd recorded two albums.

But he could see where this togetherness was leading when she invited him to her apartment one night after a session. He wasn't into Patsy that way and had to tell her as much. Tamsin had ruined him for other women.

"I hate your honesty, Cole Hawkins," she said with a bitterness in her tone. "So, 'Stranglehold on My Heart' was about her?" He nodded. "In fact all the songs you've written about the woman with the bluebell eyes were about her, right?"

"Yes. I fell in love with her years ago, and never fell out. I'm sorry, Patsy."

"So am I." Her pain sounded real. "You and I make great music together and could earn a lot of money. I could see a future for the two of us on the road."

"That's your dream, but I'm a cowboy at heart. I thought you knew that. I traveled around the country on the circuit, but the truth is, I miss home."

"And the girl you're still hung up on?" He frowned at her persistence. "When are you going to do something about her?"

"Just as soon as I get home next week."

"You're leaving that soon?"

He nodded.

"What if she doesn't feel the same way about you anymore?"

He didn't want to think about that possibility. "That's something I plan to find out."

"Would you hate me if I told you I hope it doesn't work out? You and I could be so good together if you'd give us a chance, Cole. I thought you realized I'm in love with you."

"We both love making music and have that in common, but I never saw it as anything else."

"Not ever?" she questioned.

"I was always in love with Tamsin, but you have to know I didn't mean to hurt you. All along I've been convinced you're on your way to the big time in Nashville and I couldn't be happier for you. You have an amazing talent."

"So you're going to walk out on me without even a hug or kiss goodbye?"

"Of course I'll give you a hug, and I'll be listening to you on the radio. Call me when you want to talk shop. Good luck, Patsy, but you don't need it." He gave her a warm kiss on her cheek and left the apartment. Right now only one person was on his mind. Cole's need to be with Tamsin was consuming him.

Chapter Three

By Friday, Tamsin had found a furnished one-bedroom apartment in town that suited her just fine. She took the day off from work to get settled in. Her parents were great about it when she talked to them. They'd probably wondered why a move like this hadn't happened a long time ago. But she urged them to say nothing to Sally or Lyle.

Her sister had been resting while Tamsin had made half a dozen trips to her car with her things. She would tell her and Lyle she'd found an apartment after she'd settled in. The last person she wanted to know about her plans was Dean. She wanted to get everything done and then surprise him with a homemade dinner once she told him her new address.

When he called to make arrangements for Friday night, she told him she'd be working late and hoped they could have dinner on Saturday night instead. There were still things she had to do to get ready.

Though he'd said that would be fine, she sensed he wasn't happy about having to wait until Saturday. But she'd make it up to him when he realized what she'd done.

At 10:30 p.m., she drove to the all-night grocery store a few blocks away to pick up some batteries for her remotes and some sodas. Then she was going to kick back on the couch and watch an old movie while she hung a few pictures and put books away in the bookcase.

As she was pulling a pack of colas from the refrigerated section, her gaze collided with a pair of brown eyes smoldering beneath a black Stetson.

Her breath caught to see Cole, who'd just reached for a pack of root beer to put in the cart with some other groceries, including a quart of vanilla ice cream.

Root beer floats. One of those treats they'd whipped up on many a weekend their senior year. He still loved them, apparently.

For a moment she was attacked by memories of those times when they couldn't stay out of each other's arms. For a moment she was blinded by the way his body filled out a pair of well-worn jeans and a crew neck brown shirt. Somehow he seemed a little taller in his cowboy boots than she'd remembered. Had he grown another inch?

The other night she'd noticed he wore his dark blond wavy hair a little shorter than he used to. There were more lines around his eyes. His compelling mouth looked a little harder. All in all, he was a gorgeous twenty-seven-year-old man. And she was staring at him, something she'd sworn she would never do if she saw him again. But she'd been caught doing it now.

To see the grown-up version of Cole in fire-fighter gear or otherwise sent an unwanted thrill of excitement through her body. She couldn't suppress it, no matter how hard she tried.

Tamsin guessed he was a disease she'd caught years ago. It had lived inside her all this time. What haunted her was the possibility that there was no cure. That was why she was making changes in her life. A new place to live with more privacy for her and Dean.

Cole's return to Whitebark was putting her through a refiner's fire. Her greatest fear was that Dean get trapped in it or hurt by it. When he came to her apartment for dinner tomorrow night, she would tell him some things about her relationship with Cole she'd kept private so Dean would understand.

Even if he'd been told a little about her history with Cole through his brother who would've learned it from Sally, Dean needed to hear certain details from Tamsin herself.

For the time being she didn't know where their relationship would end up. But she was hoping that living on her own, she would now have the breathing room to figure out her life. If she ended up with Dean, she wanted it to be with her whole heart and no reservations.

"I'm glad we bumped into each other."

Cole's low voice filtered through her turmoil to her brain. "It has saved me from having to find you."

To her horror she almost sighed in relief to see that he didn't wear a ring. Did it mean he wasn't married yet?

"Why would you have to do that?" she asked, trying to fight off the effect he was having on her.

His eyes narrowed between his darker lashes. "To warn you and your family that the arsonists who set fire to your barn will probably set fire to your haystacks before the summer is over."

She frowned. "You honestly think it will happen again?"

He nodded. "I was in a big conference on Tuesday with state officials. We're pretty certain why ranchers like your father have been targeted."

"Why *my* father?"

"He has always allowed hunting on his property in the fall. There's a contingent of ranchers who want to ban the elk hunters, but since they can't stop them legally, they've resorted to arson on the lands where they hunt."

Tamsin still didn't understand. "But Dad isn't the only rancher who allows it."

"That's true. So far in the last two years, sixteen ranches near the Bridger Wilderness that have allowed elk hunting have undergone losses by these arsonists."

"What's wrong with elk hunting?"

"Nothing, as long as the elk aren't transmitting brucellosis disease to the cattle when they both come to feed at the same feeding grounds. The bailed hay on your father's property, both fenced and in the barn, invites the elk to come. In my line of work, we're dedicated to eradicating the disease."

What line of work was he talking about? He was a firefighter!

She blinked. "Isn't that the disease that causes calves to abort?" He nodded. "How do you know so much about it?"

"I received my master's degree in environmental wildlife at the University of Colorado in Boulder. But my technical title is a brucellosis-feed-ground-habitat biologist, and my specific job is to test the elk for the disease. I also work for the fire department here if I'm not up in the mountains tracking elk."

Tamsin was stunned by what he'd just told her. She was having trouble taking it all in. All this time she'd accused him in her heart of going off to be a famous rodeo celebrity.

"These arsonists want the elk to migrate down the mountains away from the ranches. But the lure of the hay makes it impossible. There's a group of men so serious about stopping this, they've been willing to commit crimes like the one on your property in order to make their point."

She put a hand to her throat. "Is this happening all over Wyoming?"

"In parts where a ranch that allows elk hunting is located near a range of mountains. As you've found out firsthand, these men are endangering the lives of people and horses. After we put out the fire, I looked for you to tell you of the danger when I saw Sally. Her being pregnant makes her even more vulnerable in a situation like this and I'm afraid it's not going to stop."

His prediction increased Tamsin's fear, but she fought not to show it. "I had no idea you'd been in college all this time besides becoming a firefighter. How amazing that you know so much about what has been going on around here. How long have you been back in White-bark?"

Here she was, asking him questions when she'd promised herself she would never show him the slightest interest. Never again.

"I'd been home five days when I was called out on the fire at your father's ranch."

Only five? "Where did you get your fire-fighter training?"

"In Boulder while I was in graduate school."

Her eyes widened. "So you did both while you were there."

"Yes. When I left the ranch nine years ago, I was honoring a promise to my father that was ironclad."

"What promise was that?"

"There's a lot you don't know about the reason I had to leave. A reason my father wouldn't let anyone know about. Even on his deathbed he swore me to secrecy."

That revelation only deepened her pain. He didn't give her an explanation then, and wouldn't be giving it to her now. "What about your ranch?"

"It's still here. I'm managing with the help of Sam and Louise. You remember them?"

"Yes." Of course, she did. But how on earth could he handle everything? All this time she'd thought he'd been with that country singer, planning a new life with her. How wrong could she have been? Or maybe not. Already he'd shot her peace of mind to pieces. Before she left the store, she needed one more bit of information.

"An article about you in the *Sublette Gazette* a few months ago indicated you were involved with a country singer. Are you—"

"Patsy Janis you mean?" He cut her off. "We did a few records together. She wanted me to stay in Colorado, make records and marry her.

But I told her I wanted to go home. I take it you're involved with the man who threw his arms around you the night of the fire."

Without thinking, she said the first thing to come into her head. "That was Dean Witcom, Sally's brother-in-law."

"And your boyfriend?" After firing the question, he tipped his cowboy hat. With a rakish smile he said, "Be sure to pass on my warning to your father."

Tamsin smothered a groan as he headed for the front of the store pushing the cart. She waited until he'd checked out before she paid for her groceries. By the time she went out to her car, he'd left. After she got back to the apartment, she was no longer in the mood to watch a movie.

Cole was back and he didn't want anything from her. Why would he when she'd cut him off a long time ago, believing he didn't love her enough to stay in Wyoming?

To think he'd become a firefighter *and* a biologist!

Feeling frustrated and heartsick, she hurried into the bedroom to get her laptop. She set it up on the little kitchen table and began researching brucellosis. That led her to studying about the disease in Wyoming and its history. Never during their time together had he mentioned being interested in biology, let alone fighting fires. He'd been a bull rider for Heaven's sake!

When she'd exhausted every possible avenue of information on the subject, it was three thirty in the morning. She fell into bed physically exhausted from her move, and emotionally spent over a man who'd left her a long time ago.

He'd returned a man she didn't recognize. Tamsin didn't know how long she sobbed before oblivion took over.

Late Saturday morning she awakened to the sound of her phone ringing. She checked the caller ID before answering.

"Hi, Sally."

"Hey—what's going on? Mom just told me you moved to an apartment in town."

Tamsin sat up on the side of the bed. "Yesterday you were sound asleep, so I planned to tell you today."

"This has to do with Cole, but I don't know in what way."

"Why would you say that? I decided I needed more privacy. Getting an apartment will give me a chance to see how I really feel about Dean."

"Does he even know you've moved?"

"No. I'm going to call him this afternoon and tell him my new address. I'm going to make dinner for him."

"I know why you're doing this. It's because of Cole. Admit that if he wants to see you again, he'll be able to come to your apartment and not the house where he'd be sure to run into Dean."

"That's not true, Sally."

"You've been with Cole, haven't you?"

"No! In fact, last night I bumped into him at the grocery store. He has no interest in me anymore. I've moved on and want to concentrate on Dean."

After a silence Sally said, "I'm sorry for him and you."

"Why are you saying that? It's long past time I stopped living in the past. Isn't that what you've always said to me?"

"Yes. Forgive me. You're absolutely right to

do what you've done. Being on your own will give you the time you need to see where it's going with Dean without everyone else being around."

"Exactly. Thank you for being so understanding. Now enough about me. How are you?"

"I feel all right."

"You have an appointment with the doctor on Tuesday, right?"

"Yes."

"Please be careful. Only three more weeks and your baby will be here."

"I know. I'm going crazy waiting for it to happen."

"I am, too. I can't wait to be an aunt. Love you, Sally. Call you tomorrow."

Once they'd hung up, Tamsin decided to phone Dean and tell him where she'd moved. Over dinner she would explain her feelings.

To her relief, he answered his phone rather than it going to voice mail.

"Hey, honey—I was hoping you'd call."

"I'm sorry I've been MIA until now." She got up from the side of the bed and started pacing. "Yesterday I moved out of the ranch house to an apartment in town, and I've just finished settling in."

There was a long silence. "You *moved*?"

"Yes. I should have done it a long time ago."

"You never mentioned anything about that to me before."

"I know, but it's been on my mind for a long time. The other day I saw the right apartment for me and grabbed it."

"Why didn't you tell me? I would have helped you move."

She knew she'd hurt him. "I would have asked for it, but since this apartment is furnished, all I had to do was bring over my clothes. If you'll come for dinner, I'll explain more." Tamsin told him her new address.

There was another pause before he said, "I'd rather take you out for dinner. I'll be there at seven."

"Then I'll be ready."

"Does Chinese sound good to you?"

"Perfect."

After she hung up, her sister's observation that she'd moved so she could have private time with Cole had struck a deep nerve. It made her question her own motives. Sally had a way of doing that. If Tamsin had made this move because of Cole, it had to have been on a subconscious level. It terrified her that it might be true because that meant she wasn't over Cole and never would be!

"Tamsin—"

She gripped the phone tighter. "Yes?"

"Nothing," he murmured, before hanging up.

Oh, boy. Dean was no fool. He knew something serious had gone on for her to move from the ranch without saying a word to him.

For the rest of the day she did laundry and took a few outfits to the cleaners. When he came to her apartment at seven, she didn't invite him inside. After explaining that she was hungry, they left for the restaurant.

Tamsin knew what she had to say. It could cost her the relationship with Dean, but it was a risk she had to take in order to be fair to him. He was in a no-nonsense mood once they'd started eating their food.

"What's going on? You haven't been yourself since you broke off our date last week. Maybe you did have a migraine, but I get the feeling there was more behind it than that. I'd like to know the real reason for it, Tamsin. There's no point in pretending your feelings toward me haven't changed in some way."

She put down her coffee cup. "I'm so sorry, Dean, and I agree it's time we talked. The truth is my feelings toward you haven't changed." She sighed. "When we started dating, I told you there wasn't another man in my life. As I explained in the beginning, the only guy who ever mattered to me was Cole Hawkins, and he left Whitebark nine years ago.

"I thought we'd get married, but it didn't happen. It almost killed me at the time because I couldn't understand why he left at all if he loved me so much. The fact that he could go away and not ask me to go with him proved I'd misread his feelings and intentions.

"But a few weeks ago Heather told me something that upset me more than I would have imagined. She told me Cole was back in town…for good."

Dean's facial features sobered. "In other words, you still have feelings for him."

She shook her head. "Love has to be fed, Dean. We've been separated nine years and I heard he's been involved with a country singer. With that news I assumed that if he was back for good, it was because he was probably getting married."

He put down his fork. "Have you seen him?"

Her heart thudded hard. "Yes. He was one of the firefighters who showed up at the ranch."

"The bull rider is a firefighter now?" he said with incredulity.

"I couldn't believe it when he walked over to me in the corral and offered to stall our horses at the barn on his ranch."

Dean's mouth tightened. "You never said a word."

"I was in shock."

"Have you seen him since?"

She didn't look away. "We bumped into each

other at the grocery store the other night and had a brief conversation. He warned me about the arsonists who are out targeting some of the ranchers. He said my father needs to take precautions so it won't happen to him again."

His eyes narrowed. "Is he engaged?"

"No."

"So what does his being back in town have to do with you suddenly moving out of your parents' home and not telling me until it was a fait accompli?"

"That's a fair question. I wish I knew how to answer it."

"It's obvious you want to be with him again, and need your privacy without me coming around the ranch house all the time." Those were Sally's words exactly.

"I realize it looks that way, Dean, but honestly, I don't know what I'm feeling."

"Has he asked to see you again and pick up where you left off?"

"No!" she cried softly. "Anything but. He saw me clinging to you the night of the fire and made assumptions about us. Dean—I'm trying to figure out what's going on inside me. I wish I knew. I'm telling you this to be totally honest with you. I care for you so much and don't want any secrets between us."

"The truth is you don't love me."

"I do—but—"

"But you're not in love with me the way you were with him. Otherwise we'd be planning our wedding and you would probably have gone to bed with me by now."

She shook her head. "Now that he's back, I just need to deal with my feelings where he's concerned, but I don't want to hurt you in the process. If you can be patient with me while I get answers… You *have* to know I don't want to stop seeing you. You're too important to me. I refuse to sneak around behind your back."

He put some bills on the table to cover their meal. "I think you know exactly how I feel about you. I love you and want to get married. But when I think it's been nine years and just seeing him again can disrupt your emotions to this degree, it makes me wonder what kind of a chance there is for us. When you've finished your dinner, I'll drive you home."

"Dean—please listen to me. When he left Whitebark nothing was resolved for me. Nothing made sense. But I never thought I'd see him again, let alone get a chance to talk to him again. Now that he's home, I finally have an opportunity to confront him and I need some answers. Can you understand that?"

He pushed himself away from the table and stood up. "Yes, but can you understand that

I don't plan to put my life on hold while you make up your mind?"

"Of course I can," she whispered and got to her feet. "I'm trying to straighten out my thoughts. I hope that in being honest with you, you realize how much I care about you."

As she followed him out to the truck, Tamsin feared she'd done too much damage. "Do you wish I hadn't said anything?"

"No," he muttered. "I just wish to hell he'd never come back."

Therein lay the whole problem. A part of Tamsin was still reeling over the fact that he *had* returned.

"Dean—if you and I get married, it'll be because we both love each other with all our hearts and souls."

"But you're not there yet," he bit out.

"Seeing Cole again is like he's come back from the dead. I have to talk to him again and get certain things resolved, but it doesn't mean I want anything to change with you and me. You have to believe me."

"I'm trying."

When they reached her apartment, she opened the truck door and got out. Breaking the silence she said, "I'm so sorry. I hope you know you're the most wonderful man I've ever met. Mom's planning dinner for all of us on Thursday. I want you to come."

She was afraid that her words fell on deaf ears. He refused to look at her before she shut the door and hurried up the steps to her apartment. She could hear his tires squeal as he drove away. The sound haunted her as she reached for her phone and called Sally.

"Tamsin?" her sister answered. "It's only nine o'clock. I thought you were making dinner for Dean."

"He wanted to eat out so we ended up going

for Chinese, but he just brought me home. When I told him what has been bothering me and why, he didn't want to talk anymore. I don't blame him for being so upset."

"Neither do I." Sally was always honest. "But you can't help how you feel right now. It's a terrible situation for both of you. I'm glad you told me what's going on so I can tell Lyle."

"Your husband's going to hate me."

"No, he won't. He couldn't, even if he wanted to. He's crazy about you."

"It's a good thing I moved out. Now when Dean comes over, he won't have to face me or be worried about that. How are you feeling?"

"*So* pregnant I'm going insane."

Tamsin couldn't imagine being married, let alone knowing what it would be like to expect a baby. "I love you, Sally. Please take care. I'll call you tomorrow."

"Promise?"

"What do you think? Good night."

ON THURSDAY NIGHT Dean did come to the ranch with Lyle after work, surprising Tamsin. She hurried into the entrance hall to hug him. "I'm so glad you came."

Her mother had made stir-fry. Sally got comfortable on the couch and the six of them, including their father, sat around the TV in the family room and ate. They talked about the arson and went over the plans for the new barn with everyone adding their ideas.

Dean fit in with their family. Every look he gave Tamsin over the course of the evening told her how he felt about her. When he finally said good-night in the front hallway, she saw a new look in his eyes.

"Would it be pushing too much if I asked

you out for Saturday night? I've made plans for us."

He was being so careful, and she loved him for it. "You mean the ones I ruined last week because of my migraine? I'm so sorry about that."

"I'm trying to give you time."

"I know you are and I'll look forward to Saturday night."

"Good. Tomorrow night I have to be gone overnight in Riverton, but I'll be back the next day and phone you." His kiss was intense before he left the house.

Tamsin walked back in the living room, finding Sally alone for a minute. "Where is everyone?"

"They're helping Mom with the dishes." She eyed Tamsin with curiosity. "Tonight Dad was trying to feel me out in private and told me in his own way that Dean would make a great addition to the family."

"I've been thinking the same thing. Maybe this apartment has already given me an objective look. He's taking me out for dinner Saturday night."

"Are you sure you want to go?"

She shrugged and said, "He's trying not to push and I have to be willing to meet him halfway."

"That's good, but are you sure?"

Tamsin nodded. "He's a great person. I'd have to be out of my mind to let Cole's existence determine my life."

"I couldn't agree more."

She leaned over and gave her a kiss on the cheek. "You look tired and should get to bed. I'm going up, too. Love you." Tamsin appreciated it that her sister hadn't brought up Cole's name. It helped Tamsin, who was trying to put the past away for good.

Chapter Four

On Saturday morning Cole swung by the fire station to pick up one of the prepared fliers. They were being mailed out to ranchers, but he wanted to hand deliver one to Howard Rayburn. He'd always liked Tamsin's father and felt the need to warn him in person about this threat.

He also hoped to see Tamsin. Last week he'd left the grocery store without knowing essential things about her life…apart from her involvement with the man who'd pulled her into his arms during the night of the fire. Cole hadn't been able to get that image out of his mind. Tamsin didn't wear a ring, so at least she wasn't engaged yet. He needed to find out more about her relationship with the guy or he wouldn't be able to function.

When he pulled up in front of the Rayburn ranch house, he jumped out of the cab and hurried to the front door, anxious to make contact with her. But once again when the door opened, it was Sally he saw standing there.

She eyed him in surprise. "You're not in your firefighting gear this morning."

"No, but I am here to deliver this flier from the fire department to your father. Is he home?"

"I'm afraid not. He's in town talking to the builder who's going to erect a new barn."

"It can't be soon enough for him, I'm sure. Will you make certain he receives this?" He handed it to her. "All the ranchers in the area will be getting one, warning them that more arson attacks could be coming. He needs to take all the precautions he can."

She frowned. "That's scary news."

"I agree and I'm sorry. The police want these arsonists caught at all costs. Have you been all right since the night of the fire? It must have been frightening for you."

"I'm fine now." He could tell she wanted to slam the door in his face.

"Before I leave, is your sister home?"

"Tamsin doesn't live here anymore." Was that true, or was Sally protecting her? Both sisters had been with the horses during the fire in the middle of the night. "I imagine she's at work by now," Sally added.

"What does she do?"

"She's a CPA."

"Do you mind telling me where?"

"Ostler Certified Public Accounting."

Cole knew the location of that firm. It had been around for a long time. "Thank you, Sally. Sorry to have bothered you. Don't forget to give that flier to your father."

He heard the front door close before he reached his truck. Where was Tamsin living? His frustration grew as he drove back to town and pulled into a vacant parking spot near Ostler Accounting.

He got out of the truck and walked inside to the reception desk where a middle-aged woman was seated.

"May I help you?"

"I'm here to see Ms. Rayburn."

"What's your name? I'll ring her office, but she might not be here."

"Will you tell her it's Cole Hawkins?"

"Very well, Mr. Hawkins. Why don't you take a seat?"

He was too restless to sit, but he walked over to an end table and picked up a business management magazine they put out for clients. Tamsin had been an outstanding student in high school—she could have done anything. He wondered what had made her choose accounting.

While he stood there thinking about the years that had separated them, she came into the reception room wearing a short-sleeved suit in an apple-green color with a white crew neck top. The strappy high-heeled white sandals she had on made her look much taller than her natural five foot six.

He'd never seen her hair swept back that way. She looked classy and professional, and for a moment he was rendered speechless.

"You wanted to see me?"

She'd spoken before he'd even realized it.

Cole put the magazine back on the table and met her halfway, noticing her tiny green enamel earrings. "I stopped by the ranch to leave a flier with your father. Sally answered the door and told me where I could find you."

"You almost missed me. I have an appointment at the hospital in ten minutes."

His breath caught. "Is something wrong?"

"No. I'm going to be working on their books next week and came in to download some materials on my laptop."

Relief swept through him. "I had no idea you were interested in this kind of work."

"I thought the same thing about your line of work. Funny how two high school kids who were crazy about horses and the rodeo ended up. Truth really is stranger than fiction."

His body tautened. "What isn't funny is how

two high school kids who were insanely crazy about each other still aren't married. I'd like to take you somewhere so we can talk about that."

"The time for that kind of talk was ages ago."

"Are you engaged to Dean Witcom?"

A little pulse throbbed at the base of her throat. Emotion always did that to her. She was having trouble with his question. He waited so long for her answer, he ran out of the breath he wasn't aware he'd been holding.

"No." That one word made him euphoric. "But let's get something clear. I'll never go anywhere with you unless you promise to make a promise to me."

"What's that?"

"That you break your promise to your father and come clean about the real reason you left the state rather than stay and work things out with me. It's up to you, Cole. You know where to find me."

She wheeled around, but he caught hold of her arm so she couldn't leave, startling her.

"I'd already planned to tell you everything." The long silence had to be broken if he wanted to get on with the rest of his life. "We'll need time to talk. If it's all right with you, I'd like us to get an early start. What's your address? Why don't I come pick you up tomorrow?"

BY SUNDAY MORNING Tamsin was jumping out of her skin, partly with nerves, partly with unbidden excitement, waiting for Cole to come by the apartment complex and pick her up. After her shower, she blow-dried her hair and tied it at the nape with an elastic.

Yesterday, he'd told her to dress for the mountains. If she wanted to hike around a little, they could do that. He'd be bringing everything they'd need.

In the past they'd done a little hiking, but nothing too ambitious since participating in the rodeo had taken up the bulk of their free time. Today he was taking her to a tiny lake he'd named Teardrop, a place she'd never seen. He explained that it was at low elevation in the Wind River Range. They'd be warm and there'd be no snow.

She'd just finished her breakfast when he came to the door and knocked. Tamsin decided not to invite him inside. She was ready in her jeans, hiking boots and pullover sweater with long sleeves. Grabbing a beanie and parka, she walked out to his truck with him. It looked new.

He helped her inside and put her things on the back seat before walking around to climb in behind the wheel. This wasn't a date like they used to have. She'd come with him today for one reason only. Once she heard the true explanation about his going away, then she'd have closure and that would be the end of a life experience she wanted nothing more than to forget.

"If you get hungry, I've packed food and drinks."

"Thank you."

Cole drove them northeast to the Elkhart Park trailhead, fifteen miles from town. They were both quiet while she marveled over the scenery.

Nowhere except a few places on the North American continent would you ever see scenic waterfalls, alpine lakes, massive granite spires, high mountain cirques, glaciers and vast meadows all in one spot like this. The Bridger Wilderness was unique in the world.

He pulled onto a side road that wound

around to the little lake he'd talked about. "It does look exactly like a teardrop. What's its real name?"

"I think it's too small to have been given one. Shall we get out and walk down to the edge? I'll bring a thermal blanket."

"What can I carry?"

"Everything's in the truck bed. Have a look and take what you want."

They both got out and walked around to the rear. He lowered the tailgate and levered himself with a dexterity that had made him so exciting to watch when he was bull riding.

Tamsin saw a lot of equipment she didn't recognize. Cole handed her some water bottles. After he'd pulled a couple of loaded plastic bags from a duffel bag, he jumped down with the blanket and closed the gate. She followed him toward the water.

There was no one around to disturb their

privacy. Without a breeze, the stillness of the morning added a magical element, as if they'd arrived in a land out of time. "Did you come here a lot in the past?"

"Only a few times."

Just knowing he came here without her started up that ache in her chest.

He spread the blanket on the ground and lowered the bags to one corner. After taking the bottles from her, he put them next to the bags and sat down, removing his cowboy hat. Once he'd stretched out and rested the side of his head on his hand, she joined him.

His preference for plaid shirts hadn't changed. He wore a blue, green and white button-down tucked into jeans that outlined his hard thighs. Those long legs of his had ridden some of the toughest bulls on the circuit, winning him a lot of money.

She sat down. "Exactly how long were you on the circuit?"

"Three years before I'd made enough to start college and study to become a firefighter."

"I don't understand. Why did it take so long before you enrolled in classes?"

He sent her a piercing glance. "For one thing, I needed to pay for my mother's medical bills."

Tamsin shook her head in bewilderment. "I didn't realize she'd been hospitalized for so long. You never told me the costs had added up to that degree."

"Mother was only hospitalized a few days, Tamsin."

"But if she was so ill, then—"

"My father kept her at home," he broke in on her.

She stared at him. "I thought she died of pneumonia. Did it cost so much?"

Cole sat up and reached for one of the water

bottles. After drinking half of one he said, "What I'm going to tell you is something that no one else knows because all the interested parties are dead. I promised my father I'd keep his secret, but now I'm about to break it. Once I tell you, then only four of us will know because Sam and Louise figured it out a long time ago, but they've never said a word."

Her heart started to pound with anxiety. "Know what?"

"She didn't die of pneumonia, though that's what the coroner wrote on the death certificate. He was best friends with the doctor and they kept quiet."

Tamsin got on her knees. "About what? Tell me what you're trying to say."

His jaw hardened. "She died of undulant fever."

Tamsin closed her eyes tightly. After reading about brucellosis on the internet, she knew exactly what it was. It horrified her that something like that had happened to his mother, the woman Tamsin had only met one time.

She recalled it being an infectious disease caused by the bacteria called *Brucella abortus*. It was most often transmitted to humans from drinking raw milk from dairy cows carrying the disease, but pretty rarely these days since the advent of pasteurization. In a human it caused fever that rose and fell, sweats, headaches and generalized weakness. In livestock and wildlife, it caused the animal to abort. The disease could also be spread to other animals or humans by contact with the aborted calf.

"If you don't look too closely, the symptoms mimic the flu," he said, realizing she understood. "My mother had it all, including agonizing back pain."

Tamsin was aghast. "How did she get infected?"

"While she was helping with the birth of a cow in trouble, she wasn't aware of a cut on her forearm. It got exposed to the fluid from the cow infected with brucella."

"Oh Cole, no—" she cried. "Wasn't there a treatment for her?"

"Yes. The doctor strung it out as long as possible, but with the wrong antibiotics. He'd misdiagnosed her illness. He tried many kinds that became terribly expensive, but it didn't matter because she never recovered. Both he and Dad kept up the fiction that her pneumonia was getting worse. The doctor understood what it would mean if word got out there was a sick cow on our ranch and he hadn't realized what was really wrong with her until it was too late. No one was allowed to see her."

"So *that's* why I never got to know her after you introduced me to her."

His eyes glittered with pain. "You have no idea how hard that was for me. I told her all about you, but the doctor warned me to keep everyone away while she was dying."

Tamsin took a struggling breath. "Wasn't there a vaccine that could have made her better?"

"For the livestock, yes. And there is a cure for humans with the right antibiotics.

"But she didn't receive them and my parents were petrified. If the truth had spread, it would have set off panic in a small town like Whitebark where we were surrounded with cattle ranches. Neither of my parents could bear the thought of that. It was a source of embarrassment to Mother."

"How could she possibly have been embarrassed?"

"She felt she must have done something wrong for it to happen to her. That kind of thinking doesn't make sense, but it did to her. She didn't want anyone to know about it. The scrutiny would have been too hard for her to handle."

"Oh, the poor thing. So no one ever found out you had a cow with the disease?"

"Tamsin—we had more than one sick cow."

"What?"

"We lost a lot of calves during the calving season. Dad and Sam transported the aborted calves to the farthest boundary of the ranch and burned them before the other cattle could become exposed. No one knew about it. We thanked God the disease didn't spread to all the cows, but our herd was diminished and Dad lost his source of income."

"That's horrible."

"You're right about that. My parents held

their breath while they waited to hear of any other outbreaks, but it appeared our ranch was the only one affected that year. To my knowledge your father never had an infected one on the Circle R."

"Not that I know of, but maybe it had happened to our herd, too, and he kept quiet about it."

"I suppose that's possible."

"If he didn't tell anyone, maybe someone knew and that's why they set fire to our barn."

"No." Cole shook his head. "I can promise that's not the reason."

"How do you know?"

"There's still a lot I have to tell you. You have to understand I was sworn to secrecy about the situation and something else. Dad had no money to bury my mother and was forced to mortgage our ranch to the hilt to pay bills and keep us alive."

"Cole—" She couldn't believe what she was hearing.

"By the time I graduated from high school, there was no money left. He couldn't buy more cows to rebuild our herd and he'd developed heart trouble. It's a miracle that Sam and Louise stayed with him. They were saviors, looking after him while I had to be the one to get out there and make a decent living to save all of us and the ranch."

"So *that's* why you took off like you did!"

"Yes. Dad gave me the truck and the horse trailer. That was all he had left. Before I drove away, he made me promise I'd eventually go to college and work on a cure for that disease so no one else ever had to go through what our family did."

A gasp escaped Tamsin's lips.

"After three years of driving all over the country and winning rodeos, I gave it up, sold my horse and started classes. But I had to find another way to earn money. That prompted me to train to be a firefighter so I could draw a salary that would keep me supported while I finished graduate school.

"Even that wasn't enough, so I began selling some of the music I'd been writing over the years. It didn't bring in much revenue, but it kept me in razors and toothpaste. A year ago I was doing gigs in Boulder on my acoustic guitar on the odd weekends when I wasn't fighting fires. That's where I met Patsy. She was making records and talked me into doing a few, promising it would be lucrative."

Tamsin could hardly see him because her eyes were glazed over with tears. "And was it?"

"It could have been, but that was never my goal. After burying my father, I didn't want to do anything but go home. The minute I graduated, I didn't stay for commencement. Instead I left the rooming house where I lived, loaded up my truck and trailer and returned to get started on the rest of my life."

She turned away from him, unable to handle all the information. Nothing was the way she'd imagined. But the truth brought fresh pain. She didn't know where to go with it.

"Tamsin, it killed me when Dad swore me to secrecy where you were concerned. I couldn't take you with me without asking you to marry me. I had no way to support you at the time. Your parents wanted you to go to college and would never have given us their blessing because you didn't turn eighteen until after I left."

Tamsin knew he was right about that. "At the time, I would have gone with you no matter what if you'd begged me."

"That would have been no life for you. There

was only one way I could survive and I had to do it by winning money while I rode the circuit. If you'd gone wi—"

"I know," she cut him off, facing him again. "I couldn't have worked a job and would have been a burden that defeated the whole purpose of your leaving. With hindsight I get it." A tear rolled down her cheek. "I just wish I'd known the truth about your situation."

"If you'd known, it wouldn't have changed anything."

"How can you say that?" she cried. "As far as I was concerned, I believed you didn't love me the way I loved you."

He studied her for an agonizing moment. "After you stopped answering my letters and didn't take my calls, I decided it was better you thought that so you could get on with your life. I knew I wouldn't be back for a long time."

"I think your father was cruel to make you promise to keep it a secret from me. If you have a son one day, do you think you could ask the same thing of him? Walk away from the woman who loves him without telling her the real reason why?"

"Probably not, but nine years ago my father was in desperate straits. I owed my parents everything and had to figure out the best way to help him. If you'd read any of the letters I sent you that first year, you would know I had plans for the two of us once I started college. Though I couldn't tell you the truth of everything, I wrote letter after letter telling you I loved you, and that one day I'd be back."

She averted her eyes. "I read some of them… You asked me to be patient for three years. Once you left the circuit, you hoped I would join you and we would work things out."

"But you didn't write me back."

Anger flared inside her. "That's because I couldn't believe you would leave me. I loved you too much to let you go, but I was forced to and almost died with the pain." She took a quick breath. "So now you're going to tell me that in the end, I didn't love you with enough depth to reassure you I'd wait forever. That's what three years sounded like to me."

He shifted positions. "It sounded like a hundred to me, so I forced myself not to think about it. When I arrived in Boulder to start classes three years later, I wrote you again, but there was no answer. I was terrified I'd lost you, and I knew I was going to lose my father.

"At that point I threw myself into work day and night, praying he wouldn't die before I finished school. When that prayer wasn't answered, I had no more hope for anything that had once been important to me."

Aghast over these revelations, Tamsin got

to her feet and walked toward the lake. When she reached the edge, she started sobbing and couldn't stop. It angered her that Cole's father had destroyed their lives so a secret could be kept. She couldn't comprehend it that a father could do that to his only son, no matter how much he'd loved his wife and wanted to protect their reputation.

Mr. Hawkins could have sold the ranch. They could have moved into town and Cole could have gotten a job there so he didn't have to leave. It amazed her that his son had done everything his father had asked him to do. Tamsin never stood a chance.

If she'd left home and had gone to find Cole, he would have told her to go back without telling her why. She could see that now. His determination to carry out his father's every wish had set him on a path she hadn't been able to follow. Now it was too late with a trail of nine years' worth of lost opportunities that would never come again.

Tamsin had come with him today for answers.

You have them now, Tamsin. More closure than you ever wanted.

She wiped the moisture from her cheeks and turned around. He stood behind her, his handsome face a study in anguish.

"How am I supposed to respond now that you've told me the truth, Cole? You have my word that your secret will always be safe with me. Beyond that there's nothing more to say. Now if you don't mind, I don't want to spend the rest of the day with you. I'd rather go back to my apartment."

He stayed right where he was. "There's more I need to tell you."

"What good would it do?" she cried softly. "We've lost nine years!" The honesty poured out of her. "What an emotional waste this has been for both of us."

She walked past him. When she reached the blanket, she picked up the unopened plastic bags and carried them to the truck. He wasn't far behind and put everything in the truck bed while she climbed in the passenger side without help.

Within minutes they reached the main road leading out of Elkhart Park and headed back to Whitebark. Nothing was ever going to be the same again. Deafening silence accompanied them all the way home.

When Cole pulled into the guest parking of her apartment building, he jumped out to help her. She wanted to get away from him, but he reached in the back for her parka before walking her to the apartment on the second floor.

"You didn't need to walk me to the door."

"Yes, I did. I took this day off from work to

be with you. Let's not waste it. If it weren't important, I wouldn't ask."

"What more do you want?"

"We need to talk about the trouble your father could be facing before fall. If you'd invite me in, I'd like to explain."

"I don't understand."

"Please, Tamsin."

No, no, no. Don't let him in.

But he was being insistent. The only thing to do was to let him come in long enough to have his say.

Without comment she opened the door and walked inside the living room, putting her clothes over one of the two chairs. He followed.

"Excuse me for a minute while I freshen up. I'll be right back."

When she returned, she found him in the little kitchen drinking water from the faucet the way he used to. Some habits never went away. Tamsin could have offered him a soda, but decided not to. She didn't want him to think she desired his company any longer than necessary.

"You're welcome to use the bathroom."

He lifted his head. "Thanks."

She waited in the living room on the couch until he came back. He sat down on the chair opposite her, extending his long legs in front of him.

"I told you I was at a meeting at the fire station earlier in the week. The big brass were there. Commissioner Rich, the head of the arson squad, is alarmed by the rash of fires that have been set on ranches in this part of the county since early spring. They follow the same pattern from last year.

"Those of us assembled offered our theories. We're all in agreement that there's a group of ranchers who've been committing arson to stop the elk hunting in the county. Your father is just one of ten ranchers who've been targeted since April."

"Why exactly?"

"Because all of them allow elk hunting. These crazy guys are afraid the elk who come down to eat the hay on your property will bring more brucellosis disease to infect the cattle."

She flashed him a glance. "That's how the cows on your dad's ranch caught the disease."

"Yes. So these arsonists set the hay on fire. In your father's case, they went in the barn and deliberately lit what had been stored in there. They're determined to drive the elk away so they'll migrate down the mountains away from the cattle ranches."

Tamsin shivered. "They're desperate, aren't they?"

"Oh yes, and it's obvious the perpetrators aren't going to stop. That's the commissioner's fear, Tamsin. And mine. They're not worried about casualties. With every fire, lives and livestock are being jeopardized. My heart almost failed me to see you and Sally out in the paddock with the horses, especially when I realized she was pregnant."

"You're right. It's a horrible problem. What can I do to help?"

"Talk to your father. Let him know what's going on so he can speak to the foreman and hands on his property. They need to set up a guard rotation during the night for protection. The police are stepping up to catch these guys and put them behind bars, but in the meantime we're asking for everyone's cooperation."

She eyed him covertly. "Have you been called out every night to deal with these fires?"

"No, but that's because I'm not always here."

"How come?"

"About four to five times a month my work as a biologist takes me up in the mountains. I go for a four-day period at a time. When I come back down, I'm on call while I work on the ranch with Sam and Louise."

How did he manage it all? "What do you do exactly?"

"I've been assigned by the State of Wyoming to work in this mountain range. All winter long I catch elk and put transmitters on them so I can test them for disease. Then, the rest of the year I track the elk and study their movements to learn more about the spread of the disease. I did this on a regular basis my last year in Colorado."

"I don't see how you do that. It must be so hard."

His half smile caused her breath to catch. "Sometimes it's tricky. You have to put a GPS radio collar on the elk and use a portable ultrasound to check for pregnancy. If she's pregnant, she gets another transmitter so I can track where she calves."

She found herself fascinated by everything he was telling her. "How do you know?"

"It's a vaginal implant transmitter. If the elk aborts or calves, this transmitter pops out on the ground and you know something has happened. It's temperature activated and beats twice. I collect the transmitters and send them back to the Wyoming State Veterinary Lab. I'm in luck if I find an aborted calf I can ship off before the coyotes get it. The lab does the testing to detect brucellosis."

"Is it far where you have to go?"

"The trailheads are twenty to fifty miles away."

"But how far up the mountain?"

"This week I rode my new horse up to the

eleven-thousand-foot range to escape the mosquitos and camp out. Sometimes I fly over the area and use a handheld directional antenna in my backpack to keep tabs on them when they're out of reach."

"Do you ever have any downtime?"

"Of course. I take my guitar up and write music. Sometimes I write up proposals for an elk project, in order to apply for a grant to keep the research going. My salary is funded by hunts and angler dollars from license sales."

"You really did honor your father's wishes."

"Not the way he might have envisioned. I don't work in a laboratory to develop a cure for the disease that killed my mother. I can't be shut in. The outdoors is my home, but at least this way I feel I'm doing my part in some small way."

"Do you miss riding in the rodeo?"

"I've been too busy to think about it. I take

it you've been so busy as a CPA, you haven't looked back, either."

"You're right about that."

His eyes played over her. "Where did you go to school?"

"In Lander, but like you I worked at several jobs for a long time before I started college. Our family didn't have much money. I had to make my own way and considered myself very lucky when Mr. Ostler eventually took me on with his firm."

"He's the lucky one. You were always as smart as a whip in school." With those words, warmth swept through her. "Do you like working there?"

"Yes. Very much."

"And Dean Witcom. Do you like him?"

Her pulse sped up. "Very much."

"Does he know about our history?"

Tamsin stood up. She'd revealed her deepest

feelings about the situation with Cole to Dean and knew he wouldn't be patient much longer unless she could go to him and tell him she loved him from the depths of her soul.

"I've been honest with him about you and the other men in my life." So honest she'd hurt Dean terribly.

"How many others have there been?"

Heat filled her cheeks. "Not that many."

Cole got to his feet. "Does he want to marry you?"

He did, but she didn't want to tell Cole everything. "Yes."

"How long have you known Dean?"

"A year, but we only started dating four months ago. He and Lyle are close."

"If you get married, that would be a nice arrangement. Two brothers and two sisters who love each other. I always wanted a sibling, but it didn't happen."

Cole sounded so reasonable—and for a moment, so lonely—she wanted to die.

"Thank you for the warning. I'll be sure to talk to my father before today is out. He has no idea what you've uncovered and will be grateful for the heads-up."

"I'm the one who should be grateful to you for coming with me today. I wasn't sure you would. Despite what you think, if you want to know the truth, I needed this time to talk to you more than you can imagine."

Why? Tell me—what aren't you saying?

But he didn't answer that question.

In the next breath, Cole left the apartment. After he descended the outside staircase, she watched him stride to his truck from the living room window. When he drove away, it was like déjà vu. He'd taken her heart nine years ago—and just now he'd taken it again.

But this time he'd left her with no promise of

phone calls or letters asking her to be patient until they could be together one day. It was too late for them. He knew it and she knew it.

Tamsin had done enough of that to last a dozen lifetimes. She was *so* through with re-living the last nine years of waiting for a future with him that had never come that she hurried into the kitchen for her purse. Once she left the apartment and reached her car, she drove to the ranch at full speed. On her way in the house she ran into her mother who was sweeping the kitchen floor.

"Hi, honey. How's it going at your new apartment?"

"I love it." She kissed her cheek. "Is Dad around?"

"He's outside with the contractor."

"I need to talk to Sally, but when the con-tractor leaves, I have to talk to you and Dad for a few minutes. It's important."

Her mom got that wishful look in her eyes. "Is this about Dean?"

Sorry, Mom. "No. It's about the fire, but I'll explain later." Not wanting to get into anything else, she hurried down the hall to the bedroom and knocked on the door.

"Come in."

"Sally?" She found her sister lying on the bed reading a book.

She put it down and stared at Tamsin. "Judging by the state you're in, you've been with Cole."

"Yes."

"And?" she prodded.

"It's over. I mean it's really over."

"No, it's not. You can't see your eyes, but I can. I have news for you. It was *never* over."

Tamsin sat in a chair near the bed. "He drove us to the mountains to talk. I finally have answers as to why he left Whitebark without taking me with him."

"Seriously?"

"Their family was in a desperate financial situation. Cole was sworn to secrecy and couldn't tell me anything. He had to go on the rodeo circuit to make money in order to save the ranch and pay the bills. His father was in bad health with a heart condition that was growing worse."

"Oh, Tamsin. That's awful."

Tears stung her eyelids. "I'm still furious that his father forbade Cole to tell me the real reason I couldn't go with him. All these years I've thought he didn't love me."

Sally sat up in bed with effort. "Did he admit he's still in love with you?"

She took a deep breath. "No. And I can tell you right now that I haven't been on his mind, not for years. You wouldn't believe everything he's done since he stopped riding the circuit."

"Is it bad?"

"Not at all. Today I learned that becoming a firefighter was something he did to make money while he went to school."

"School—where?"

Tamsin kneaded her hands. "If you can believe, he got his master's degree in biology at the university in Boulder."

"Biology?"

"Shocking, isn't it? I'm still reeling."

"Why in Heaven's name would he get a degree in that?"

"I was as surprised as you are. He's taken a job working for the State of Wyoming to control brucellosis disease among the elk in the Winds."

"That's so weird, you couldn't make it up."

"My thoughts precisely. Let me explain." For

the next few minutes she told her everything she could, only leaving out the personal tragedy that had afflicted Cole's life. She followed up by telling her the reason for the arson and why their father needed to provide safeguards so it wouldn't happen again on their ranch. "I'm going to be talking to Mom and Dad about it later today."

"I can't believe what I'm hearing."

"You're not the only one. But this is such a serious problem, you and Lyle have to help me convince Mom and Dad that you're not safe until these crazy arsonists are caught."

"Good grief." Sally eyed her with an anxious expression. "Okay. Now that you've managed to convince me you're telling the truth, what did you learn about Patsy Janis? Don't tell me you didn't discuss her because I wouldn't believe you."

Sally was way ahead of her. Tamsin sat forward. "I told him I'd seen an article in the paper about the two of them. Before I could ask questions, he cut me off by explaining that she wanted him to stay in Colorado and make records with her, but he told her he wanted to get home. When I asked him if she wanted to get married, he said yes."

"I see. Did you tell him Dean wants to marry you?"

"Yes."

Her sister let out a frustrated sound. "I'm glad you told him. Being dishonest doesn't get anyone anywhere. But the point is, we both know you could never love Dean the way you love Cole."

"You used the wrong tense." She got up from the chair. "I'm not in love with Cole anymore. In fact, I could never love a man who fights fires for a living. You never know if he'll come home from another fire. When I remember what happened to Mandy Epperson's father, I can't imagine how awful that would be. It's no way to live. I refuse to do it."

"Tell that to your heart. Tamsin, do yourself a favor and find out for sure. The next time he wants to be with you, don't hold back no matter how much you hate what he does for a living."

"What do you mean, next time?"

Sally rolled her eyes. "There'll be one. But this time, be open and honest with him about Dean, the way you wished he'd been with you nine years ago about his real reason for leaving. If the two of you are meant to be together forever, then you need to find your way back to each other. Honesty is the first step."

"Cole had the chance to be honest. He said he'd wanted to tell me about his family crisis and admitted he'd needed the chance to explain. Well—he explained, but he said nothing about his personal feelings."

"Did he try to kiss you?"

"Are you kidding? Even when he came into my apartment, he didn't try to make any moves."

"Did you give him the chance to get closer?"

"It wasn't like that." Tamsin averted her eyes. "He didn't look at me like he used to. I told Dean I needed to talk to Cole. But now that I have, there's nothing more to learn."

"So where does that leave you with Dean?"

"I don't know." She half moaned the answer. "I told him that if we get married, it will be because I love him with all my heart and soul."

"Oh, Tamsin. You're in a very bad place."

"You're right. I'm a mess. Maybe I'm not destined to be married. If I continue to be confused, then I need to set Dean free so he can

find someone to love who will adore him. I'm thinking I won't ever get married, but that's okay."

"What do you mean by that?"

"On my way over here I decided I'm going to go after more accounts. If I devoted my spare time to picking up some new clients in Lander and Riverton, I could double my income so I can finally branch out on my own. My goal is to own my own business one day and I'm going to make it happen. The sooner the better."

ON LATE THURSDAY afternoon of the following week, Cole came back down from the mountains. After stalling his horse, he phoned Chief Powell to let him know he was back for the next four days. Then he walked in the kitchen to find Louise fixing dinner for her and Sam.

"Good to have you back, Cole. While you were gone, you had a visitor."

His heart thudded unexpectedly. *Tamsin?* She'd been on his mind day and night since he'd left her apartment last Sunday. He hadn't begun to tell her all the things in his heart. If she was in love with Dean, then she wouldn't want to hear any of it.

He walked over to the fridge and pulled out a cola. "Who was it?"

"Patsy Janis."

Frustration caused his hand to squeeze the can so tightly, he was surprised it didn't pop open.

"She's staying at the Whitebark Hotel and said she wouldn't be leaving until she'd heard from you."

The top hotel in the town. Patsy never quit. When he'd ignored her message, she hadn't

let that stop her. He took a swig. "How long has she been here?"

"She came to the door the day before yesterday in a rental car."

With some women you could say goodbye and they would get the message. But not Patsy. She'd come to Whitebark knowing he was a firefighter and had asked enough questions to find out his ranch address.

She'd been gutsy from the time she was a talented teenager with a desire to be the best country singer in the business. If she wanted something, she went after it and was determined enough not to tip him off with a phone call.

She might want Cole. He knew part of her did, but she had an agenda, one he wanted nothing to do with because he didn't love her. Her plan that they would be a husband and

wife team, singing around the country making records, had been a dream of hers alone.

"Thanks for telling me, Louise. I'm going
to take a shower, and then I'll head into town
and let her know I got the message."

"Is she someone important to you?"

Louise rarely pried, but if anyone had
the right to know things, it was the faithful
woman who'd given his father loving care all
those years.

"Patsy's a friend in the music world, nothing more. As you know, there's only been one
woman for me all these years. I'm working on
doing something about that."

A smile broke out on her face, indicating she
liked his answer, before he left the kitchen for
his bedroom and drained the rest of the can.

She and Sam had known how much he'd
loved Tamsin. He knew they'd always liked her,
too, back when he used to bring her around.

But that had been at another time of life, a time that had come to a painful end and was long since over.

The sophisticated Tamsin of today had emerged a gorgeous, savvy businesswoman who was going to marry Dean Witcom. This was the price he had to pay for those years of silence he was forced to keep because of a promise to his father.

What did you expect, Hawkins? That she'd come running into your arms?

He'd imagined it in his dreams. But he was awake now. Dreams be damned!

After he'd shaved and cleaned up in jeans and a shirt, he took off for town. If he couldn't find Patsy at the hotel, he'd wait for her—unless or until he got a call on his beeper and had to take off.

He parked along the street and walked inside to talk to the man at the front desk. "Would you please ring Ms. Patsy Janis's room? My name is Cole Hawkins."

"Yes, sir."

After a short wait the clerk said, "She's not answering."

"In that case will you leave her a message that she can find me in the bar unless I have to respond to a fire?"

"What's your name again?"

"Cole Hawkins."

The man wrote it down and put it in one of the boxes. Cole headed for the bar and grill to order a meal. He hadn't eaten since coming down the mountain earlier. Now he was hungry and needed food in case he was called out on a fire.

Summer had brought the tourists to the Winds. While Cole ate his meal, he looked around the crowded bar in case he spotted Patsy, but no such luck. She'd been in several magazines lately, touted to be an up-and-coming country star by the media.

She was blonde, sexy and talented—she turned heads, that was for sure. But not his. Tamsin had his heart, pure and simple.

The minute he finished a second cup of coffee, his beeper went off, ending his opportunity to tell Patsy she'd wasted her time coming to Whitebark. Since he presumed she'd flown all this way, he would rather have told her as much in person, though he had zero desire to see her. But now he would have to say it over the phone the next chance he got.

He put some bills on the table and charged out of the hotel to his truck. Within a minute he reached the fire station parking lot and ran through to the locker room to pull on the set of hurry-ups he kept here.

Wyatt had already climbed on the back of the ladder truck when Cole jumped on and the truck took off with the siren blaring. It wasn't long before they arrived on the scene at Kyle Drive. Captain Durrant told them that an evergreen tree had caught fire and ignited the eaves of the house. The fire got into the attic and did significant damage to the roof.

Between the four of them, they doused the flames. Whoever lived there had been out of the house at the time. But the captain found it suspicious that a green, healthy tree had caught fire. It sounded like shades of arson but couldn't be proved until the arson commander investigated further.

While they were outside cleaning up, Cole saw a man drive up in front and get out of a truck with a WDOA logo. He'd seen that truck before in front of the Rayburn ranch house and assumed it belonged to Sally's husband. But of course there were other people employed by the oil company.

Cole and the others did the rest of the cleanup and returned to the station to reload and change their equipment.

"Hey, Hawkins?"

He turned to Steve Perry, one of the other firefighters. "Chief Powell wants to see you in his office."

"Be right there."

On his way, he grabbed some bottled water and had drained half of it by the time he entered the room. But the chief wasn't alone. A man he hadn't seen before sat near his desk. Commander Rich, the captain and the other guys from the ladder truck were also gathered.

"Thanks for coming, Cole. Sit down." He found a seat. "Mr. Hawkins? Everyone else has been introduced. This is Mr. Witcom, production manager at Witcom-Dennison Oil. The captain said that you and the crew put out the fire in the attic at his house. At this point we're certain it was arson and wonder why he might have been targeted."

Cole was dumbfounded. That fire had been started at Tamsin's boyfriend's house? His thoughts flew ahead. If she married Dean, they'd likely be living there. Cole was stunned by the coincidence and got a pit in his stomach that wouldn't go away. First her father's ranch. Now her lover's?

He studied the man who'd held Tamsin in his arms the night of the fire. Cole had to admit the guy would appeal to most women. Judging by the size of his house, he made a substantial income. Cole had never known jealousy before. This was new to him.

"I thought he should hear from all of you about the arson being committed here in the county since April. There might not be a link, but every suspicious fire is worth investigating."

Witcom's blue eyes narrowed as he stared at Cole. With that look, Cole knew in his gut Tamsin had told him about their history. How much of it, he didn't know. No doubt Witcom didn't like the idea that Cole had shown up back in Whitebark after all these years.

Once again everyone gave an opinion of what they thought and saw. Then it came to Cole's turn. "The only observation I could add might not have any relevance."

"Go on," the chief urged.

"The Rayburn ranch was targeted a couple of weeks ago. Mr. Witcom was there at the scene because he and Ms. Rayburn are a couple."

Everyone looked at the man in surprise. Cole hated to be the one to reveal that private kind of news, but this was an official investigation. No doubt Witcom was close to despising him now.

"Maybe they decided to target him in order to send another message. We know these arsonists hope to frighten ranchers like Howard Rayburn to close off their ranches to elk hunters come fall."

The chief nodded. "It could be a possibility. We'll look into it. Thanks, everyone. You're excused."

Cole avoided looking at Witcom and walked through the station with the other guys to change out of his gear. Once he'd put on his jeans and shirt, he walked out the back door and headed for his truck, totally gutted to have laid eyes on the man Tamsin was seeing.

Chapter Five

"Hey, cowboy!"

Cole's head lifted. He knew that sultry female voice. "Patsy?" It shouldn't have surprised him to discover her standing next to his Ford. After what had happened tonight, this was all he needed.

She'd pulled her rental car up next to him. A smile broke out on her face. "I figured I might not see you for some time if I didn't drive over here." She went where angels feared to tread, but she'd made a mistake this time.

"You're probably not aware this is a private parking area."

"Well, it's good to see you, too." She started toward him, but he put his hands on her shoulders and kept her at a distance.

"I don't know why you're here, but this isn't the place for a conversation. I'll drive back to the hotel and wait for you in the bar."

After letting go of her, he got in his truck and backed around. Unfortunately, a couple of the guys reporting for duty had seen them, but there wasn't anything he could do about it and drove out to the street. She wasn't far behind.

He found a spot near the hotel and hurried inside to let her know how he felt about her unwanted presence. Instead of a table, he sat at the bar and ordered coffee. Within minutes she'd joined him.

"It's clear I shouldn't have come to your work."

Cole turned to her. "You shouldn't have come to Whitebark. The last time we were together I told you I wasn't in love with you. I had fun jamming and recording with you, but it never turned into love. I realize those weren't the words you wanted to hear. Now I've come home to my life and am asking you to go back to yours."

The bartender brought him coffee and took her order for a beer. While she drank some, she flashed him a glance. "I didn't know there was this side to you. I think you really mean it."

"You know I do."

"You're so angry, I take it your girlfriend hasn't forgiven you and doesn't want you back. That's what I came to find out. I think I have my answer. Things really aren't going as smoothly as you'd hoped. What do you know…"

He'd had all he could take.

"Patsy—I'm in love with her and I don't want to hurt you. You've got a great career going. We'll always be friends, but you're wasting your time coming here."

"But we made a good team, Cole. This woman you love obviously doesn't want you back. Doesn't it mean anything to you that I want to be the new woman in your life and love you?"

He drew in a breath. "I'm flattered, but it wasn't love for me even though we had fun making music together."

"Wow. She really did a number on you."

"I've been in love with her forever. Good-bye, Patsy."

Cole left the hotel. Before he went back to the ranch, he drove straight to Tamsin's apartment. Her Toyota was in her parking space. He hoped that meant she was home. He needed to see her before she heard from someone else that Patsy had been in town. Some of the guys at the station had seen them together and word got around fast. Too fast.

After pulling up in front of the complex, he got out of his truck and raced up the stairs to her apartment. Without knowing her cell phone number, he had no other choice but to go there.

He knocked on her door and waited. When she didn't respond, he knocked a little harder. He knew for a fact that she wasn't with Dean right now, but she could have been with him earlier. After the fire that had broken out tonight, Cole could count on Witcom driving over there any minute to tell her he'd come face-to-face with Cole and how he felt about it. But more important, he needed to warn her that the arsonists were so serious they'd targeted Dean.

In case she was nervous to say or do anything this late at night, he called to her. "Tamsin? It's Cole. I know it's late but I have something vital to tell you. If I'd had your number, I would have phoned you first. Tamsin? Can you hear me?"

Seconds later she opened the door looking beautiful and anxious. She'd dressed in jeans and a T-shirt that hugged her curves. "What's wrong? Was there another fire?"

"Yes, but not at your family's ranch."

She put a hand to her mouth in obvious relief. "Come in."

He walked past her, hearing noise from the TV in the background, and waited until she'd shut the door. "Tonight a lodgepole pine next to Dean Witcom's house caught on fire and the flames burned his attic."

A small gasp escaped her lips. "Was he hurt?"

"No. He didn't come home until our crew had put it out and was ready to leave. Chief Powell called a meeting at the station afterward that included Witcom. It's too early in the year for the tree to be dry enough to burst into flame without help. Since there was no lightning tonight, the only way to explain the fire is arson."

A troubled expression broke out on her face.

"We have no proof yet, but are thinking there could be a connection to your father's barn fire since you're his daughter and are involved with Dean. The chief asked for opinions and I had to tell him what I was thinking. But I don't think your boyfriend was too happy about it coming from me of all people."

She sank down on the couch. "So you really believe he was targeted too because I'm Howard Rayburn's daughter?"

"It's a strong possibility. I just wanted you to know so you can tell Witcom to be careful. I don't think he would have liked that advice from me. Have you talked to your father yet?"

"Yes. He's doing everything possible to stay on alert."

"That's good." He shifted his weight. "One more thing before I go. Patsy Janis was waiting for me at the back of the station after tonight's fire. I never thought I'd see her again."

Those blue eyes trapped his. "Why not? You said she wanted to get married."

His jaw hardened. "But I told you I didn't feel that way about her. The truth is marriage takes two willing people who love each other. I told her I'd meet her in the bar at the hotel where she's been staying. A couple of the guys at the station saw her with me. I figured it was only a matter of time before you heard gossip about it.

"We had our little talk at the bar. After I told her I was never in love with her and this had to be goodbye, I walked out without looking back. If she ever comes near me again, she won't be welcome."

Tamsin jumped to her feet. "Why would you think I wouldn't believe you?"

"Because of all the fake news in the magazines and newspapers being printed," he broke in on her. "The truth is, I'm not and never have been involved with Patsy intimately no matter how much she wanted to get married," he informed her. "Ours was a professional relationship. Period."

He headed for the door.

"Wait—"

Cole looked over his shoulder.

"Don't leave yet."

"I'd rather not be here when Witcom shows

up. I'm surprised he hasn't come yet." He opened the door.

"If he were going to come over, he'd phone me. I—I need to tell you something first," she stammered.

He stood there with the door still ajar. "What is it?"

She rubbed her hands over womanly hips in a nervous gesture. "For what it's worth, I haven't told Dean I'll marry him."

The blood pounded in Cole's ears. "Are you saying you're not in love with him?"

Tamsin averted her eyes. "I'm saying that I haven't told him I'll marry him yet. He wants to get engaged, but I'm still trying to sort out my feelings."

That was the best news he'd heard since he'd left Whitebark years ago.

"If nothing's set in stone, does that mean you'd be willing to spend some time with me?" His heart thudded while he waited for her answer.

"I don't know if it would be wise."

"Why? I'm home for good. Are *you* planning to leave the state?"

She threw her head back so he could see her eyes. "I have no idea where my career might take me."

Encouraged by those words he said, "Until you do know, how would you like to go to the Arapahoe Pioneer Days Rodeo in Lander with me coming up in a week? Or do you have plans with Witcom for the Fourth of July?"

It appeared his question had caught her off guard. "We haven't talked about it yet," she muttered.

"I'm leaving in the morning to head back to the mountains for my work and will probably be gone for five or six days this time. If you decide you'd like to go to Lander with me, drop by the ranch and tell Louise. She'll let me know after I'm back.

"I was thinking we'd drive there on the fourth and spend it camping overnight in the Setons' backyard. Their daughter, Doris, and son-in-law, Tyler, have invited me. We'd be sleeping in a tent in our sleeping bags. Sam and Louise's fifteen-year-old grandson Jake Sky Tree is riding in the relay. They exchange horses after each lap. It's pretty exciting. Then he's competing in the rodeo and there'll be fireworks afterward. We would drive home the next day.

"If there's no message from you when I get back, then I'll have my answer. Good night, Tamsin. Please be careful and lock your door after I leave."

WHAT WAS IT Sally had told Tamsin?

The next time he wants to be with you, don't hold back.

What do you mean, next time?

There'll be one. But this time, be open and honest with him about Dean, the way you wished he'd been with you nine years ago about his real reason for leaving. If the two of you are meant to be together forever, then you need to find your way back to each other. Honesty is the first step.

Sally had predicted that Cole would approach her again and she'd been right. Tamsin couldn't lie to herself. His invitation had thrilled her to death. But the fear of getting involved with him again scared her out of her mind.

After the years of emptiness while she'd fought her memories, to start that whole thing all over again would be a form of insanity. Of course no one knew what the future held. She wasn't asking for a guarantee, but to spend time again with Cole meant she had to be some kind of fool and hadn't learned that she couldn't go back to their senior year of high school when they'd been crazy in love. It wasn't possible to know that kind of happiness a second time.

By the time she'd turned off the TV and had gone to bed, she was glad Cole had given her time to think about his invitation instead of wanting an answer right away. But before she fell asleep, she knew she wouldn't be going by his ranch. She also knew something else. She didn't love Dean the way he needed to be loved. It truly was over with him.

Maybe a man would eventually come into her life, one who would set her on fire in a brand-new way. Until that day came, she would go ahead with her plan to build her own CPA business.

Thank goodness she'd moved out of the ranch house. Soon her sister would have the baby and they'd move to their own place. After that there'd be little chance of running into Dean when Tamsin went home to see her folks.

With a plan in mind, she left for the office on Friday morning, eager to talk to Heather before she left for Whitebark Hospital to start their audit. Her friend arrived after Tamsin did. She rushed over to her.

"I'm glad I caught you before I had to leave. What are your plans for tomorrow?"

"Nothing special, but I have a date with Silas Ellsworth to go to dinner and a movie."

Tamsin remembered him from high school. "You've been seeing a lot of him lately. Sounds like it could be something serious."

"Maybe." Her friend smiled.

"How would you like to drive to Riverton with me for the day? We'll be back in time for you to meet up with Silas. I want to check out possibilities for some new clients."

"You mean for yourself?" she whispered.

Tamsin nodded. "It wouldn't hurt to try to pick up business, even if it means a move. I don't want to work for someone else forever."

Heather frowned. "But I thought that you and Dean…well, you know…"

"I'm afraid that's over, but I'll tell you about it when I have more time. Give me a call later if you want to go with me."

"I will, I promise."

Tamsin grabbed her briefcase and left for the hospital. But no matter what else she had on her mind, she couldn't stop her glance from straying toward the mountains. They were Cole's world when he wasn't ranching or fighting fires. He was probably halfway up to the area where he'd be searching for elk over the next week.

His ability to be on his own in nature was remarkable to her. He'd always been a fearless cowboy. Now he was up in the remote wilderness of the Winds facing dangers and loving every minute of it.

That ache in her heart would always be there because he was a man who didn't need a woman. He'd proven it over the last nine years. Tamsin wished with every atom in her body that she were a woman who could exist without a man and be happy. If it was possible, she intended to find out.

By midafternoon her cell phone rang. She presumed it was Heather, but when she checked the caller ID, it was her mother. She clicked on.

"Hi, Mom."

"I'm glad you picked up. Guess what? Your sister is in labor and Lyle has driven her to the hospital. Your father and I will be driving there as soon as he comes in."

This was the best news Tamsin could have received. "She's been so good obeying doctor's orders, but it's past time her ordeal was over."

"I agree. Where are you?"

"Would you believe I'm at the hospital doing an audit?"

"What a lucky coincidence!"

"I know. I'll finish up here and go to the maternity floor."

"We'll see you there soon, darling."

As soon as they hung up, Tamsin called Heather to tell her about Sally. "I'm going to have to change my plans about driving to Riverton tomorrow. Will you go with me next Saturday?"

"I can't go then. Our family has plans that

weekend and I've invited Silas. Let's do it in two weeks."

"That will be perfect. Talk to you soon," she said.

"Let me know all the fun news about the baby."

"I want to hear about Silas, too."

"Of course."

They hung up.

The audit would take several more days. Since Tamsin couldn't concentrate on debits and expenditures right now, she planned to pick up where she'd left off when she went back to work on Monday. Now that the files were downloaded on her laptop, she packed it in her briefcase and walked through the hall to the bank of elevators.

On her way down to the maternity ward on the third floor, she realized she'd be seeing Dean at some point and wasn't looking forward to it. But it was something she would have to deal with now and in the years to come when there was a reason for both families to be together.

Still, her heart sank when she ran into him as she came out of the elevator. He took one look at her and pulled her aside. "I need to talk to you before we go in to see Sally and Lyle."

Because Cole had come over last night, she knew what Dean was going to tell her about. "Let's go into the waiting room."

They followed the signs that led them around the corner. Several groups of people were sitting in the room on the chairs and getting drinks out of the vending machines.

Dean found them a couple of chairs and they sat down. "Last night someone set fire to my property. The fire department believes it was the same arsonist who set fire to your father's barn."

She nodded. "I heard."

"After the meeting at the fire station, it didn't take Cole Hawkins long to inform you, did it?" he said in a wintry tone. "I saw a truck outside your apartment and figured it was his."

So he *had* come by without phoning her. When she ignored his comment, his lips tightened. "Lyle said Sally doesn't know about it, and we don't want her to know."

"I agree she doesn't need to be worried about anything but having their baby."

He got up so fast it surprised her.

"Wait—" She caught hold of his arm. "I'm so sorry for what happened to you, Dean. I heard the damage was confined to the attic, not the whole house, thank Heaven, but it's still awful. What a shock that must have been!"

"The bigger shock was coming face-to-face

with the guy I hate." In a pain-filled voice he said, "Excuse me. My brother needs me right now."

Without giving her a chance to say more, he walked away. She stood up and followed him down the hall to the nursing station where they were given directions to the labor room.

When they walked in, a worried yet excited Lyle reached for his brother. Tamsin hurried over to the hospital bed. "Sally—" Her sister looked drained and exhausted. "I can't believe it. When did the pains start?"

"Last night. But the doctor says the baby won't be born before evening."

"That long? Oh, you poor thing."

"You have no idea." She rolled her eyes in that way of hers.

"Mom and Dad will be here soon."

"I know. Did you come with Dean?" she mouthed the words.

"No."

Sally closed her eyes. Another contraction had taken over her body.

"You're the bravest woman I know."

Her sister let out a groan.

A few minutes later two sets of parents came into the labor room. Tamsin hugged her parents and left the room before she had to face Dean's parents. She'd only met them once. If they knew what had happened between her and Dean, then they wouldn't be thrilled to have to talk to her until it was absolutely necessary.

Tamsin headed for the waiting room with her briefcase. She would sit out there for the next few hours. Until her little niece was born, she could work on the audit from her laptop. But after a few minutes, she couldn't concentrate. It upset her that all she could think about was what it would be like to be married to Cole and have their baby.

"Tamsin?" She lifted her head, surprised to see Dean standing there. "I'm leaving. I'll come back when the baby's born. You can go in and be with your family now."

"Dean—" she called after him, filled with guilt because she'd hurt him, but he'd disappeared too fast. If she'd gone after him, what would there have been to say? Nothing that would make him feel better. She didn't love him enough to marry him and he knew it.

WEDNESDAY NIGHT OF the following week, Cole returned from the mountains in a rainstorm and headed straight for the shower after taking care of his horses. He was glad to be out of it. When he walked into the kitchen later to make a peanut butter sandwich, he found Louise and Sam enjoying a cup of coffee.

"I thought you two would be taking off for Lander today."

Sam shook his head. "The rain stopped us from going, but it's supposed to clear up before morning. We'll head out then."

"After I take care of a few bills in the morning, I'll drive there later in the day."

They talked about ranching problems for a little while, but it was clear Tamsin hadn't dropped by. He ate his sandwich and swallowed it with a half quart of milk before saying good-night.

Once he'd gotten ready for bed, he put his beeper on the night table, hoping he wouldn't be called out on a fire. He hadn't had a decent night's sleep since leaving Tamsin's apartment. Over the last six days, Cole had hoped she'd thought about everything and wanted to be with him. But his worst fear was realized tonight when Louise hadn't mentioned her name.

The next morning he awakened to a tap on his door.

"Louise?"

"Sorry to bother you. We're just leaving. I would have let you sleep longer, but you have a visitor waiting for you in the living room. It's Tamsin. What shall I tell her?"

He leaped out of bed so fast, he stubbed his toe and let out a moan. "Ask her to wait. I'll be there in a few minutes."

"Okay."

Cole had to be the first man who ever shaved and got dressed in under a minute. He strode through the ranch house to the front room and found the woman he loved studying some small framed photographs of his family on one of the end tables. "What a surprise to see you here."

She turned around to face him, looking stunning in jeans and a tan Western shirt with fringe. "I wasn't sure you would be back until I saw your truck parked at the side of the ranch house." After a slight hesitation she said, "Last week I had no intention of seeing you again."

Why didn't she tell him something he didn't know. "What happened to change your mind?"

"Sally had her baby girl a few days ago."

"That's terrific. Is everyone okay?"

"Yes. Little Kellie took her time being born, but they're both healthy and happy. When I was alone with my sister at the ranch yesterday and she asked me if I'd seen you lately, I told her there'd be no point. She shook her head and said, 'So it's truly over with you two?'

"Without answering her question, I told her I had to go and would talk to her later.

As I walked out of the bedroom she called to me. 'Did you know ostriches don't bury their heads in the sand? They're much more likely to face a problem head-on, which makes them wiser than one particular human being I love.'"

A smile broke out on his face. "Your sister is a very intelligent young woman. I take it you've decided to drive to Lander with me and face our situation head-on."

"If the invitation still stands."

He had to tamp down his excitement. "How soon can you be ready to go on an overnight?"

"I'll need to drive back to the apartment and pack a few things, including my sleeping bag. It won't take me long."

Cole checked his watch. "It's ten thirty. I'll be by your place at noon."

"Be sure to bring your guitar and pack some of your recordings. I'd like to hear them."

"With Patsy singing? I don't think so." He wanted no reminder of her. "I only provide backup guitar."

"Her singing won't bother me. I want to hear the songs you composed in the mountains. Will you let me listen to those? Please?"

Her brilliant blue eyes begged him. "I'll see what I can dig up."

"Good."

"We can grab some lunch at a drive-through before we leave town."

"Sounds great. I'll be ready."

He'd been ready for nine years. After walking her out to her car, he hurried inside and rushed around to pack and load the truck. One of his dreams was about to come true.

The bills could wait for a couple of days. Knowing that Sam had given the stockmen their instructions, Cole could leave the ranch with no worries. He left his beeper by the bed, grabbed his guitar and left through the back door to reach his truck. Louise gave him a thumbs-up on the way out.

This trip could be the making of them. *Or the breaking*, a little voice nagged. Cole refused to listen and took off for her apartment. She didn't trust him. Somehow he had to prove that he would never fail her, but that meant she had to stick with him long enough until she knew the truth of his love for her in her heart.

When he reached her place, she was waiting for him outside her door with her cowboy hat and boots on. It reminded him of their rodeo days. He took the steps two at a time to grab her overnight case and sleeping bag. "You don't look a day older than when we were in high school."

"Thanks, but we know that's not true and

we can't go back to those days, Cole. I know I don't want to."

The trail to her heart was riddled with obstacles. He would have to proceed with great care from here on out. After putting her things in his truck, they drove to Hilda's for a hamburger. Cole remembered she liked pickles, mustard and a fresh limeade. But after what she'd said a few minutes ago, he wasn't going to make any assumptions about the past. Instead he asked her what she wanted.

"A beef taco and a cola."

He ordered his usual triple-stack cheeseburger with ketchup, fries with fry sauce and a frosted root beer and paid for everything. She shot him a glance. "I can see your eating habits haven't changed."

Amused, he said, "I thought you didn't want to be reminded of the past."

She looked away. "My mistake. I'm sorry I was rude to you earlier."

"No offense taken." He drove on to the pickup window for their food, then found a place to park while they ate.

"Has there been any word yet about the arsonists responsible for the fires?"

"Not that I've been told. I know they're working on it. I'll learn more the next time I'm called in. We can be thankful no lives were lost in the last two fires. Did you talk to Witcom about the one at his house?"

"Briefly."

"Do you mind if we discuss him for a minute, Tamsin?"

She finished her cola. "There's nothing to say. Unless he happens to be around family, I won't be seeing him again."

"Because of me."

He heard her take a sharp breath. "Because

seeing you again proved to me I was still holding back with Dean. If I'd been in love with
him the way I was with you, I'd be engaged
by now. Nine years ago I would have done
anything to be with you. I was ready to run
off with you and defy my parents.

"The truth is, I've never loved Dean with
that same intensity, but it took your coming
back to Whitebark to make me see what was
wrong. So it's better that I've broken it off
completely."

Chapter Six

That was what Cole had been waiting to hear. Seeing her in Witcom's arms the night of the fire had practically destroyed him.

"But the timing of the baby and the fire at his house haven't made it easy for us since we've been forced to see each other one way or another," she added.

"That's tough." He didn't tell her that in time it would be easier to see Dean when he came around the family, since he wasn't certain it would be.

She turned to him. "Was it tough dealing with Patsy again?"

"No, because unlike your feelings for Dean, I never felt an attraction to her or thought I might learn to love her. I've only ever been in love with one woman."

He ate his last french fry. "Did you want to get anything else to eat? Otherwise, I'd like to get going."

"Nope, I'm ready."

He started the truck and backed out. Before long they were on the highway headed for Lander. The rain had greened up the mountains below the timberline. He had a sense of well-being as he breathed in the fresh clean air. Cole hadn't felt this alive and invigorated in years. There was only one reason why. She was sitting next to him.

To Tamsin's chagrin it was happening. She could feel it. The old magic that had been in hibernation for nine years had sprung to life once more, suffocating her with feelings and sensations she couldn't suppress. Cole was back. Already he was coloring her world again.

During their two-and-a-half-hour drive, he turned on the radio, but she turned it off and asked if she could listen to some of his recordings.

"I brought one. It's in the glove compartment."

She reached for it. Patsy Janis was featured on the cover in a cowboy hat, holding the microphone. The woman was beautiful and sexy. She found it amazing that he hadn't fallen for her.

Tamsin turned the CD over and studied the

list of six titles on the back. Lyrics and music composed by Cole Hawkins.

She gasped softly as she read each one. "Doomed to Love Her." "Her Bluebell Eyes." "Stranglehold on My Heart." "Never a Reply." "Lost to the Winds." "Wind River Lovin'."

Cole—

Years ago he'd told her she had eyes the color of the bluebells growing in the Winds. As she read each title again, she realized it was a history of their relationship. But "Doomed to Love Her" said it all. He'd described her state of mind.

Unable to look at him, she slid the disc into the CD player. Patsy's crooning voice filled the interior of the cab. She was a great singer, but it was Cole's music and words with his guitar accompaniment that made their way inside her soul.

She'd expected his music to have that free,

easy, on-the-road kind of feeling. But nothing could be further from the truth as they headed for Lander with the Wind River Mountain Range filling their vision. "Doomed to Love Her" reached right into her soul.

Next came "Her Bluebell Eyes." It was so beautiful and mournful at the same time, the words squeezed her heart.

Their eyes met for a breathless moment before the third song came on.

You know what you do to me,
You know what you do to my heart,
Your stranglehold loving,
Sets our love apart.
You know I'll never be free, babe,
You know I'll never stray.
I'm always here for you,
Until my dying day.

"Cole—" she cried softly.

It seems forever since we held each other tight,
So long since you told me of your love,
So long to smell your fragrance in the night.
So long since our kiss at first light.
You know I'll never be free,
You know I'll never stray,
I'm always here for you, darlin',
Until my dying day.

With those words, Tamsin broke down and quietly sobbed.

"If you ever wanted to know my feelings, you know them now. Those were the words I wrote to you in my letters."

The letters she'd refused to read.

She couldn't talk as the next two songs came on. "Lost to the Winds" and "Never a Reply" almost tore her heart out. But it was when the last song came on that she really lost it.

Remember the day we had to part?
Those broken dreams that stomped on my heart?
Gone were the days of laughter,
Gone were the nights of joy,
The end of Wind River lovin' ripped my soul apart.
Remember the years of longing, of waiting,
Trying to pretend everything was all right?
Remember the mornings you could taste the salt from your tears?
The dying inside with each passing night?
Too much pain at the day's start?
The end of Wind River lovin' destroyed my heart.

To her surprise, when she finally lifted her head, she discovered he'd turned into a rest stop and had reached for her, pulling her close. His shirt was all wet from her tears. She hadn't been held by him in nine years. Tamsin was so in love with him, she couldn't breathe.

Needing to compose herself, she eased out of his arms and sat back on her side of the truck. The emotions she'd experienced listening to the CD had drained her. He started the truck and they took off once more.

Cole turned on the radio again, but she asked him to turn it off. "Your songs are incredible. You should be out there making more records and performing before a live audience."

"I appreciate the compliment, but that's not my goal in life. I enjoy composing. If one of my songs gets recorded by a great band, that's terrific, but I'm finally where I want to be. That's never going to change. And today I'm with the woman who makes me happy."

Tamsin shook her head. "We haven't made each other happy in years."

"I've had my memories."

So have I.

"Are you ready to make some new ones? We've reached Lander. After we stop by the Setons' and set everything up, it'll be time to hit the Buffalo Barbecue. Then we'll all head over to the arena for the rodeo."

She swallowed hard, trying to find her voice. "I haven't been to a rodeo in ages. Do you wish you were performing?"

"Do you?" he fired back.

"No. For once it will be fun to watch."

"Sounds good to me. I'm getting too old for that kind of fun."

She couldn't imagine him ever being that old.

He drove them to the Setons' home, a charming rambler with a big backyard and patio.

Farther on was a barn and corral. But what stood out to Tamsin was the fabulous tan-colored tepee erected on the grass. Someone had decorated it with hand-painted horses and it stood at least sixteen feet high.

She helped Cole carry their gear where they would set up the tent. "Who painted their tepee? It's fantastic!"

"Doris. She's an artist and sells her artwork at the Arapahoe Marketplace in town."

"I'll have to buy something from her."

"You can tell her that yourself. She'll be so happy."

When Tamsin turned, she saw four people walking toward them. She knew Sam and Louise, but not their daughter, Doris, or her husband, Tyler. Cole introduced her to them.

"We're so glad you could come. Our son Jake is so excited. He wants to be a great bull rider like Cole one day. He's over at the arena practicing."

Tamsin smiled at her. "We're looking forward to watching him perform in the rodeo. In fact, we can hardly wait. But now that we're here, I want to know about the artwork you do. I've just moved into an apartment and would love to buy something of yours. Cole tells me you're an artist, and anyone looking at the tepee can see your work is outstanding."

"Thank you. I paint a lot of pottery and wall hangings."

"Well, before we leave town tomorrow, we'll go by the shop."

"Cole said you wanted to camp out, but feel free to come in the house at any time to use the bathroom and fix yourself some food or a drink."

"That sounds terrific. If you don't mind, I'd like to go in right now." She turned to

Cole. "I'll be back in a minute to help set up the tent."

His piercing brown eyes played over her, not missing an inch. It sent a rush of desire through her body. "There's no hurry."

Doris showed her inside. Once she was refreshed, she walked down the hall, but paused in front of a deerskin wall hanging. It was obviously something Doris had painted. Tamsin read the words of the quote.

Everything an Indian does is in a circle, and that is because the power of the world always works in circles, and everything tries to be round. The sky is round and I have heard the earth is round like a ball, and so are all the stars. The wind in its greatest power whirls, birds make their nest in circles, for theirs is the same religion as ours. The sun comes forth and

goes down again in a circle. The moon does the same and both are round. Our tepees were round like the nests of birds. And they were always set in a circle, the nation's hoop. Even the seasons form a great circle in their changing, and always come back again to where they were.
—Chief Black Elk

Stunned by the last sentence, Tamsin read it a second time.

The seasons always come back again to where they were.

Was that what she and Cole were doing? Coming back to where they'd begun? Was their love part of the eternal circle? If she'd read this nine years ago after he'd left without her, she would have considered it so much nonsense. But right this minute it made so much sense, it sent chills racing up and down her spine.

"What a beautiful saying and artwork."

"Thank you. We live by it."

Tamsin thanked Doris and hurried outside as if a ghost were chasing her. Cole had been out to this house many times. Had he noticed the wall hanging and read it? Of course he had.

When she reached him, he'd already erected the four-man tent and was chatting with Tyler. She shouldn't have been surprised he'd done it so fast since it was something he did every time he went up in the mountains. She grabbed her sleeping bag and went inside to lay it out.

Cole had put his duffel bag on one side with a couple of lanterns, leaving her plenty of space. But the fact remained that they would be sleeping under the same roof tonight. That was something they'd never done before, but only because Cole had never tried to take advantage of her.

All she had to do was go back outside for her overnight bag, but he brought it in for her, blocking the doorway to the tent with his tall, hard-muscled body.

"When I told you we'd be sleeping outside, I should have offered to set up another tent. It's in the back of the truck. If you're uncomfortable sleeping in here with me tonight, I can do that or I can stay in the tepee."

Tamsin kept thinking about that quote on the wall in the Seton home. Maybe the power that moved the world was working on her. "I'd like to sleep in here with you tonight. It's one of the few things we've never done."

His eyes narrowed on her features. "A new memory to make," he said in a husky voice that caused a fluttering sensation in her chest.

She felt heat rush to her face.

"Shall we go get some dinner before we head to the arena?"

Cole followed her out the door of the tent and walked her to the truck. They drove to the city park where a huge crowd had gathered. The Buffalo Barbecue never disappointed. They filled their plates and sat at a table under the canopy with Sam and his family while they enjoyed the music and entertainment.

Jake joined them, but he monopolized the conversation with Cole, wanting any last-minute tips he could give him. Tamsin loved the camaraderie with their family. Cole had grown up with them. When she thought about the two losses in his life, it touched her that the Setons treated him as one of their own. She had no doubt it filled the hole in his heart so that he hadn't been forced to come back from Colorado to an empty house.

When she tried to put herself in his place,

she couldn't. If she'd been gone for years and had to come home to a ranch devoid of her family... She couldn't begin to imagine it. But Sam and Louise had been there for Cole when he'd needed them most. They'd guarded his secret and had taken care of his ailing parents. Without knowing them, she loved them for their goodness.

To Cole's satisfaction, Jake placed fifth in the marathon and second in the teenage bull-riding competition. He gave him a bear hug. "You keep working on it. Next year you'll be number one." Tamsin gave him a hug, too, putting a smile on his face.

The fireworks thrilled everyone far into the night. At ten after twelve, Cole left the park happier than he'd been in years. His thoughts were all over the place by the time he and Tamsin arrived back at the Seton house.

With a three-quarter moon in a sky free of clouds, they saw their way clearly as they walked around to the backyard.

Cole went on ahead to get the lantern from the tent while Tamsin darted inside the house for a minute. When she came back out, he'd lighted it and followed her over to the tepee where she was examining the horse paintings.

"Doris is an amazing artist, Cole. Every horse is a different breed or color. Out here in the moonlight, the tepee looks surreal, like we've gone back in time. I love it. If my parents had one of these when I was young, I would probably have slept in it a lot."

His gaze roved over her face. "We can sleep in it tonight."

"You mean it?" He could tell she was excited by the idea.

"Of course. Let's get our things out of the tent and move in here for the night."

"They won't mind?"

"Tamsin—whenever I drive here, I sleep in it. The tent's a pain to set up."

She chuckled. "So you did all that for me? Why didn't you say so when we first arrived?"

"I didn't know how you'd feel about it."

"After reading the quote on the wall hanging in the house Doris painted, I'll feel honored to sleep in here tonight. With that moon up there, the whole night seems enchanted."

He felt it, too, and walked to the tent to get their gear. She helped him and, before long, they'd entered the tepee large enough to house a family. The floor was laden with gorgeous Arapahoe-designed rugs, and there were several low, rustic divans and log drums that served as end tables. The fire pit in the middle would keep you warm in the winter.

Her eyes followed the line of the poles that

rose through the hole at the top. "I had no idea the interior would be so elegant."

Cole nodded. "This tepee is made of elk skin and gives it a richness that canvas never could."

"No wonder you always sleep in here when you come. It's pure luxury."

One of the things he loved about Tamsin was her appreciation for life. She'd shown a graciousness to Sam's family plus a friendliness to Jake that he knew had pleased them.

"While you get ready for bed, I'll say goodnight to everyone and then I'll join you." He reached in his duffel bag for a pair of gray sweats and left the tepee. A few minutes later Cole emerged from the house having changed clothes. He was more than excited to spend the night with Tamsin. This was a first for them. It could blow up in his face. But now that he was back home after a nine-year separation, he didn't plan to waste a second with her.

The soft light from the lantern bathed Tamsin in a special glow. She'd already climbed inside her sleeping bag and lay on her side with her head on the pillow.

Cole stretched out his bag a few feet away from her. But after pulling a pillow from the duffel bag, he walked over to her. Once he'd dropped it next to hers, he lay down outside her bag and lowered his mouth to hers, stifling her surprised cry.

At first she tried to wriggle away, but he'd trapped her with his arm around her body, drawing her as close as he could with the bag between them. The taste of her mouth after all his dreams of loving her almost gave him a heart attack.

He drove his hungry kiss deeper and deeper until he heard her satisfying moan. Then there was no more protest as she began to kiss him back in the old familiar way. Cole felt like they were eighteen again, but this was so much better because circumstances had changed. At twenty-seven years of age, they were free to love each other with no more obstacles.

The ecstasy of being able to let go of long suppressed emotions caused him to forget time. Their desire caught fire so he was trembling. "I always wanted to sleep out under the stars with you, but it never happened," he lamented against her lips.

"We were underage, Cole."

"Our age had nothing to do with it and you know it. We couldn't keep our hands off each other. I wanted to make love to you from the moment we met, but the time wasn't right. If I hadn't had parents who needed me desperately, I would have run away with you and lived with you until we could be legally married."

"We're both aware of what went wrong, Cole. I don't want to revisit the pain of the past. Please let's not go there."

"Never again." He tasted salt and realized it came from her tears. "Why did you agree to come here with me?"

He had to wait for her answer. "Sally challenged me to find out if I still loved you. I fought her at first, but when I see the happiness she shares with Lyle and their excitement over the baby, I decided I needed to be certain before I said a final goodbye to you."

"Thank God you did," he whispered against the softness of her neck. "I love you, Tamsin. I always have, and I always will." He lifted his head and looked down into her eyes. "I only need to know one thing. Do you love me?"

Tamsin searched his brown eyes that burned

with desire for her. "You know I love you, Cole, but I don't dare give my heart to you again."

He caressed the side of her face. "How can I prove to you that I'll never do anything to hurt you?"

"You can't." She turned her head to kiss his hand. "It wasn't your fault that you had to leave Whitebark. I know that now, and I know you never loved Patsy. But circumstances beyond our control drove us apart before, and they're doing it again."

A frown marred his striking features. "What are you talking about?"

"Do you remember that terrible forest fire in the Winds the year you and I were dating?"

"Of course. My father provided backup."

"Then you remember that my best friend Mandy lost her firefighter father while he was battling it."

"That was a very sad day. I remember going to the funeral with you."

"Exactly. Eight other firefighters from the county also died after getting trapped. It was so horrific, neither Mandy nor her family ever got over it. Five years ago they moved to California to be near relatives and get away from the pain. I haven't seen her since."

He blinked in confusion. "What are you getting at?"

Tamsin gripped his hand. "I don't want to go through that, Cole. Loving you once was hard enough. But to love you again and be terrified every time you get called out on a fire—" She shook her head. "I couldn't do it."

He sat up, alarmed. "So if I ask you to marry me, you'll turn me down because I fight fires?"

She averted her eyes. "Are you asking me?"

"You *know* I am."

"Then I'd have to say no," she said in a broken voice. "If we had children someday, I wouldn't want them to have to go through what happened to Mandy and her family."

"That will never be the case," he muttered.

"I'm sure Mandy's father told his wife the same thing. But you can't make a statement like that, Cole," she fought back. "I thought you were a cattle rancher, but you came home from Colorado a biologist committed to working in the mountains at least half of every month. That I could handle. But it isn't enough for you. When you're home, you're fighting fires. I want a man who's home with me every minute he can be."

"Will you marry me if I resign?"

Her breath caught. "No, because in the first place, you're following in your father's footsteps. Everything he's ever asked of you, you've done like an obedient son. Even if you could break a promise to your father, I wouldn't want you to do so for me. I couldn't live with you knowing you'd made that kind of sacrifice. You'd learn to hate me. That's the one thing I could never live with."

Chapter Seven

Tamsin's words had gutted him. Cole got to his feet. "So what you're saying is we're doomed not to have any kind of relationship."

"I guess I am, but I'll always love you."

That wasn't good enough. "I'm going to ask you again. Why did you come to Lander with me?"

"To get my head on straight."

"And now you think you have?" Cole stared

down at her. "That's it? In twelve hours everything's clear, cut and dried for you?"

"That's how it felt when you left Whitebark."

"So what you're really doing is paying me back for all those years of pain?"

"No, Cole! I shouldn't have said that. I didn't mean it the way it came out."

"The hell you didn't. When I wrote 'Doomed to Love Her,' I never dreamed I was writing a self-fulfilling prophecy."

In the next instant he reached for his pillow and bag.

"Wait—please don't go!"

"There's nothing you could say that could make me stay. Good night, Tamsin. We'll head for Whitebark in the morning." He turned out the lantern and left the tepee, but she raced after him. When he reached the tent, he started to zip the screening.

"Don't shut me out!" she cried, and pushed

her way inside before he could do it up all the way. The momentum launched her against him and his arms went around her so she didn't fall.

For a moment their bodies were locked together. She clung to him. "We need to talk, Cole."

"We already did that. It didn't work…but since you're here, I plan to kiss you into oblivion." Faster than she could believe, he swept her into his arms and laid her down on top of his sleeping bag. Then he joined her, locking her legs with his so she couldn't move. He plunged his hands into her hair and found her mouth.

"Cole—"

His name was all he heard before he smothered any other sounds and began to devour her. He'd done enough thinking about them for a lifetime. This was the only way to get through to her.

"I love you, Tamsin, but since you've cut us off at every turn, we can at least take advantage of this night. I know you want me, and Heaven knows I want you. I'm too on fire for you to stop now. If this is all we will ever have of each other, then let me make love to you as if tonight was our wedding night. In my heart you've always been my wife."

She made a sound that could have been in protest or something else, but it no longer mattered. He rolled her on top of him, craving this closeness more than he needed air, and kissed every feature of her face.

"Do you have any idea how beautiful you are? I couldn't count all the dreams I've had about you. Don't deny us the pleasure of this night. It's going to have to last us for the rest of our lives."

At first she seemed to be with him all the way. Her hunger matched his as they got caught up in a rapture too marvelous to describe. But suddenly she tore her lips from his and pulled back, placing her hands against his chest.

He groaned. "Don't pull away from me now, sweetheart."

"Cole…we have to stop before we can't. I'm going back to the tepee."

His breath caught and he grasped her arm. "Surely you don't mean that."

She refused to look at him. "I followed you inside here to talk to you and explain everything that's going on inside of me."

"We *are* talking in the most elemental of ways."

"You know what I mean."

His temper flared. "I never thought of you as a tease."

She threw her head back. "If you think that's what I'm doing, then you never knew me. You couldn't possibly understand how terrified I am of losing you in a fire. I've never seen you back down from a challenge. That's what made you such a great bull rider. You've never been afraid of anything in your life."

"That's not true. Every firefighter has to deal with fear. But we compartmentalize it differently."

"I don't know how you do that. When I saw you in your firefighter gear and realized what it meant, I was panicked and horrified. Don't you realize that horror has grown worse over the last few weeks? What if our positions were reversed, and I was the firefighter and you the CPA? How would you feel knowing that every time I went out on a call, disaster could strike and I might not come back in one piece to you and our children?"

He took a deep breath. "I'll admit I'm glad I didn't come home to find out you were a certified member of the fire department. No doubt it would tear me to shreds if I watched you pull on your turnout gear."

She let out a tormented sigh. "Oh, what's the use of going over this? We'll never get anywhere."

"Tamsin? I have an idea for us to meet each other halfway."

"What do you mean?"

"As soon as I came home from Colorado, Chief Powell took me on without question. I feel an obligation to him. At the time I had no idea how you felt about this."

"I realize that," she muttered.

"Over the years I'd had talks with my dad. He impressed upon me at a young age that it was important to be an integral part of the community. That's why he became a firefighter and helped when he could. I never recall my mother being upset by it, but it's possible she felt exactly the way you do."

"You never got frightened when your dad went on a call?"

"I was hardly aware of it. He was a rancher first, and later on he had to slow down. When I look back, I can see how lucky we were that he never had a serious injury that made a deep impression on me. If he did, he never said anything about it."

"I don't understand what you're getting at."

"When we get back to town, I'll have a talk with Chief Powell and tell him the truth. Once he hears that I want to get married, but being a firefighter is getting in the way of our plans, I'll make him a proposal."

"What kind?"

At least she was listening. "That I stay on until the arsonists are caught. Every man in the department is needed. Once the culprits have been identified and arrested, then I'll leave the department. We're hoping this menace will be shut down by next month. Can you give me that much time to work things out?"

"No." She half moaned the word.

"I see." He rolled away from her. "Since you couldn't have made that any clearer, I wish you'd go back to the tepee now."

The next thing he knew she'd draped herself over his back, and pressed her cheek next to his. "I didn't mean that I couldn't give you the time you needed before you quit. I was saying no to the idea of you giving up your job permanently for me. It isn't right."

"Look, Tamsin. This isn't a matter of right or wrong. I'm willing to compromise in order to marry you, yet I can see it's still asking too much of you."

"That's not true!" She moved around so she

lay face-to-face with him. Her hand crept into his hair. "If you can give it up after the arsonists are caught, then I'll do my part to make our marriage work. My salary at Ostler's will cover what salary you give up and I'll help with the ranching. I love you too much to lose you, Cole."

He raised up on his elbow, having been elevated from the depths to the heights so fast, he was out of breath. "You're not going to change your mind?"

She pressed a hungry kiss to his mouth. "I wouldn't do that to you."

"In that case, don't move." He sprang to his feet and lit a lantern.

"What are you doing?"

He smiled. "Wait and see. Close your eyes."

"Cole—"

"Just trust me."

"I do," she said emotionally.

What a glorious sight she was in navy blue sweats with her disheveled hair gleaming like chestnuts and her lips swollen from his kisses! He reached in his duffel bag and pulled out the little velvet box he'd packed. Cole had been operating on faith, having bought her a ring after finding out she wasn't engaged.

He pulled it out of the box and got on his knees in front of her. "Now you can open them."

When she did, he reached for her left hand. "With this ring, I'm making our engagement official. Be sure this is what you want because I won't let you give it back." He slid it home.

Her eyes had turned into moist blue pools of light. "After waiting nine years, you can be sure I'll treasure this forever." She stared at the ring. "I love this diamond. It's in the shape of Teardrop Lake."

They'd always been on the same wavelength.

"When the jeweler showed me the different cuts, I was immediately drawn to this one for that very reason and asked him to set it in yellow gold."

Her smile lit up his universe before she threw her arms around his neck and kissed him long and hard. "I adore you, Cole."

Being with her like this had made him euphoric. He pressed her back against the pillows. When they finally came up for air he said, "If I'd run off with you long ago, I couldn't have given you a ring or offered you a life."

She burrowed her face in his neck. "Let's not think about the past."

"Agreed. We've got a future to plan. The first thing I want to do is let Sam and Louise know we're engaged. They'll be overjoyed for us."

"I believe they will, and I want to thank them for letting us stay here."

"We'll do that. When we get back to White-bark, we'll drive to your parents' so I can ask them for your hand."

"They're old-fashioned. They'll love it."

He kissed her mouth passionately. "After that we'll get my horse trailer and go pick up your mare. She can stay in my barn. From now on let's spend all our time off together whenever possible."

Tamsin hugged him with surprising strength. "It's like a dream. I can hardly believe this is real." She held up her hand to look at the ring again, but dazzling as it was, it couldn't match the glow in her eyes.

"There's a lot more to come. I want to walk through the ranch house with you and get your ideas. By the time we're married, I want it re-furbished and ready for us. Sam and Louise have always had their own apartment with us, but it's asking a lot of you. I don't know how you feel about that."

She caught his face in her hands. "They've been your family for a very long time. In time I hope they'll include me in theirs."

Overcome with emotion, Cole crushed her to him. "You couldn't have said anything to make me happier. I love them and love you for feeling the way you do."

"I already love them because it's very clear they love you." She kissed the line of his hard jaw. "Do you think you can plan some of your work for the state to be done over weekends? If you do that, then I can go with you and help you look for elk."

"I'm planning on it."

"I wish we were married right now."

"But we're not, so I want you to get inside my sleeping bag."

"Cole?"

"I plan to be your husband when I make love to you for the first time, so don't tempt me."

"But a minute ago—"

"A minute ago I was a desperate man!" He stood up so she could get under the covers. Once she was settled, he stretched out next to her and pulled her close. "Help me to control my desire for you, Tamsin. I can live until we're married, knowing you have my ring on your finger. I just want to hold you for the rest of the night. Keep on hugging me, sweetheart. I've needed you for so long. Never let me go."

TAMSIN KNEW BETTER than to argue with this extraordinary man who'd just asked her to marry him and had given her such a beautiful ring. Cole Hawkins had more integrity than anyone she'd ever known. He'd proved it in ways that had caused her to wade through rivers of sorrow, but that was all in the past now.

She remembered what her father had once said to her after Cole had gone away. *I know it's no consolation right now, honey, but mark my words. One day the right cowboy will come along.*

Letting out a sigh, she closed her eyes and nestled as close to Cole as she could. Like Chief Black Elk, her father had been a prophet, too.

Twelve hours later she reminded her father of those words after she and Cole had arrived at the ranch. When they pulled up to the house, her dad was just helping her mother out of the car. It looked like they'd just come home from church.

Tamsin got out of Cole's truck carrying a couple of small packages and ran over to hug them. He followed her. "I'm so glad you're home!" Tamsin cried.

"How are you, honey?"

"Wonderful, Mom."

"Cole? It's good to see you." They shook his hand. Her parents had kept their opinions about Cole to themselves, but she knew deep down they were anxious for her now that she'd gone on an overnight with him.

"Did you have a good time in Lander?"

"It was an incredible experience. Sam and Louise's teenage grandson is becoming a top bull rider, just like Cole."

"That's really saying something," her father responded.

"They also have a daughter, Doris, who is a fabulous artist. She sells her artwork at a shop in town. Cole and I stopped by there on our way home. I bought the two of us some of her pottery and a doll for Sally to give the baby when she's older. Doris made it from buckskin with a beaded dress and high-top beaded moccasins. I can't wait for you to see everything."

Her mother lit up. "This is exciting! Let's go in the house so I can see it. I'm afraid Sally and Lyle are over at his parents' house with the baby this afternoon, but they'll be back soon." The news filled Tamsin with relief. It meant Dean wouldn't be anywhere around.

Once they'd gone into the living room, her father said, "Welcome back to Whitebark, Cole. It's been a long time."

"Too long. There's no place like home."

"Indeed there isn't. You're all grown up. I'm glad I finally have a chance to thank you for helping save the ranch house from catching fire. Wouldn't you know those arsonists did their worst while we were away on a trip?"

"They have a way of knowing when to strike. I was so relieved that no one was hurt."

"You can say that again."

"Tamsin said you're taking precautions in case they try to cause any more trouble."

"I read that brochure you brought to the house. We're on the watch for them."

"That's good to hear. We've been asking every rancher near the Bridger Wilderness to be extra vigilant."

Tamsin put Sally's package on an end table and handed the other one to her mother. "Here, Mom. Open it."

Inside was an eight-inch turquoise watering pot shaped like a bird with a yellow comb and a picture of a yellow sun on both sides with the rays trailing. The pot had little yellow feet.

"That's the cutest pot I've ever seen!"

"I think it is, too. I bought a watering pot shaped like a dark red buffalo with yellow feet and yellow drawings on the sides. She makes all her own pottery. You should see the tepee around the back of their home. Doris painted all kinds of horses on the elk skin. Each one is a work of art.

"In her house she's painted a wall hanging I covet." Tamsin flashed a private message to Cole. "I want one just like it."

A half smile broke at the corner of his mouth. "Maybe that can be arranged."

Her mother put the pot down on the coffee table. "Have you two eaten? You're welcome to have dinner with us."

"We'd love to, but Cole needs to get back to his ranch. Before we go, we have something important to tell you."

"It couldn't have to do with that diamond on your finger, could it?" Her dad didn't miss much.

"What?" her mother cried.

Tamsin held out her hand. "Cole asked me to marry him last night."

The man standing next to her slid his arm around her waist and pulled her close. "I've loved her from the first moment we met in high school. We'd like your blessing."

Her parents looked stunned. Tamsin knew what was going through their minds. Only days ago they'd supposed she and Dean might end up together.

"Of course you have it!" her mother cried and hugged both of them. "How soon should we be planning your wedding?"

"We're still working that out," Cole explained. "It can't be soon enough for me."

Tamsin eyed her father through moist eyes. "There's only one thing you need to know, Dad. Whether you believe it or not, I listened to the advice you gave me nine years ago. Do you remember what it was?"

He nodded with a smile. "I told you that one day the right cowboy would come along."

She beamed. "You're looking at him."

To her joy, her father gave Cole a hug. "Welcome to the family. In a way it's like you've always been a part of us, but it has taken a hell of a long time to make my daughter's eyes shine like they used to."

Tamsin could tell her father's words had touched Cole. He put his arm around her again and squeezed her hip as her parents walked them out to Cole's truck. She waved from the open window.

"Don't forget to give Sally the doll. I'll call her later tonight and tell her our news. Love you."

As they drove away, Cole grasped her hand and kissed it. "I'm surprised your mom and dad were so accepting of me."

"If you want to know the truth, I'm positive they've gone back in the house jumping for joy. Their lovesick daughter has just been cured of a disease she came down with nine years ago. It's been touch and go ever since."

Cole's rich, happy laughter filled the cab's interior. It seemed like forever since she'd heard that full-bodied sound. But when his phone rang, she was brought back to reality knowing he had to answer it. The conversation didn't last long before he hung up.

"Which work needs you most?" she teased.

"There was another fire last night, this time at the Naylor ranch. He owns more property than anyone else around and has that private runway on his ranch that brings in elk hunters from all over the country. The arson commander has called a meeting with the brass. In fact, it has already started. Chief Powell took a chance I was back from Lander. I have to be there."

"Let's go to the station right now. I'll drive to the apartment. When you're through, call me and I'll pick you up."

"Thanks for understanding. If it doesn't last long, we'll drive to the ranch for my horse trailer. I'd like to bring your mare back tonight."

"That can wait. We'll do it after my work tomorrow."

He nodded and drove fast to reach the station. The ladder truck was out in front, ready for the next run. After pulling to a stop in front, Cole reached across the seat to kiss her. "I love you," he said before levering himself from the cab. By the time she got out and walked around to climb behind the wheel, he'd disappeared inside.

Tamsin was glad the department was having another meeting. The sooner they caught the arsonists, the sooner he would give up fire-fighting and they could get married.

COLE WALKED INTO the conference room while Holden Granger was talking and found an empty seat in the back. The chief nodded to him.

"With the help of Norm Selkirk, head of County Law Enforcement, we've discovered the name of one Sublette County rancher who has made many trips to the eastern border of Wyoming this year and last to buy gasoline. Norm saw a pattern and started checking all the towns from Gillette and Newcastle to Lusk and Cheyenne. The rancher's actions are highly suspicious since he has to cross the state each time, but I'll ask Norm to give you the details."

The other man stood up. "Thanks, Holden. We've pinpointed this man because he made all his purchases in February and March of both years. He's been very clever to only go once to any one station. We've discovered he used a silver 2010 Dodge Ram 3500 one-ton truck with a fifty-gallon auxiliary tank an arsonist could use. But consider that it was three years ago."

That sounded about right to Cole. One of those ugly duallies.

"What makes this case so difficult is that none of the ranchers whose property was targeted ever saw anything suspicious. So how did this arsonist spread the accelerant so fast without anyone being aware?

"I talked to a convenience store clerk in Torrington who remembered the guy because the machine outside couldn't read his credit card. He had to bring it inside and while they chatted, the clerk said the man mentioned he needed gas for his generator in case the power went out.

"We know who this cattle rancher is, but his identity has been protected by state law. After some further investigation, we've learned more. Three years ago, brucellosis was confirmed in his herd of cattle and his ranch was put into quarantine, but it was kept quiet."

Cole could relate. The news often set off panic amongst other ranchers.

"Those cases stemmed from exposure to diseased elk, of course. I was able to talk to the state veterinarian. She was able to identify the prevalence of brucellosis.

"The quarantine held until the positive cattle were identified and euthanized. After three different inspections of the rest of the cattle that turned up negative, the quarantine was lifted. We have reason to believe this man had a strong revenge motive and is the one responsible for committing arson along with some helpers. But we don't have proof until we catch him in the act."

He sat down and Holden took over once more. "We've identified the other cattle ranches in our area near the Bridger Wilderness that could be their next targets. Last night four sets of haystacks set on fire at the Naylor ranch are a case in point. One of them caused a grass fire that burned twenty acres."

Cole had gotten engaged last night, thus missing that fire. He found it incredible that the arsonists had been so brazen. But it didn't surprise him.

"With the help of the forest service and other law enforcement agencies from the bordering counties of Lincoln and Teton who can add manpower over the next month, we're doubling patrols of the vulnerable areas here. I'll leave the last word to Commander Rich."

The older man stood up. "I can't tell you how important it is that we stop this man in his tracks. You men are on the front lines in this war zone. If you see or hear anything in the days to come—something that sends up a red flag—Sheriff Granger needs to hear about it immediately. He's manning our communication center."

Once the meeting disbanded, Cole phoned Tamsin to come and get him. Until she arrived, he chatted with some of the guys out by the ladder truck. While they were discussing what Norm had told them, an idea came into his head and it wouldn't let go. He couldn't wait to get out of there and do some investigating on his own.

When Tamsin pulled up in front, he climbed in the passenger side and leaned over to kiss her cheek. "Will you drive us to your apartment? I want to spend the rest of the evening with you more than anything, but something came up at the meeting I have to take care of, so I'll drop you off. Tomorrow when you're through with work, we'll grab a bite to eat and get your horse stalled in my barn."

Much as he would like to share his thoughts with her, he couldn't. No one could know what he was up to.

"I should have known our little holiday was too good to last, but I'm not going to complain. You've made me too happy."

"Tell me about it." He caressed the back of her neck beneath her silky hair. Cole wanted her for his wife and needed to solve this arson case ASAP.

"I talked to Sally while I was waiting for your call. She told me she always knew I would end up with you."

He grinned. "Do you think there's a chance she'll stop hating me one day?"

"If you asked her that question to her face, she would tell you she wished she could have hated you all these years. It would have been a lot easier than having a crush on you from a distance."

"You made that up."

She laughed. "No, I didn't. She said to tell you welcome to the family at long last."

He chuckled. "Did you talk to Lyle?"

She shook her head. "I decided it was better she tell him first. He'll know what to say to Dean. By the way, Sally adores the doll I bought for the baby. She wants me to take her to that shop one day soon."

"We'll plan on it."

Too soon they pulled up in front of her apartment. Darkness had crept up on them and clouds obscured the moon. Cole jumped out and hurried around to lift her from the driver's seat. This way he could envelop her in his arms and kiss her thoroughly before he let her go.

"Call me tomorrow when you get a minute," he whispered against her lips. "I'll be out mending fences with Sam."

"I'll need your new phone number, remember?"

"Amazing that we've managed this long without them." After another deep kiss, they programmed their cell phones and she hurried up the steps to her apartment. He waited until she was safely inside to turn on lights and had come back out to wave him off.

He waved back and sped through town to reach the ranch in record time. Sam's truck was parked around the side. They must have come back earlier and left a light on for him.

As soon as he unloaded his gear from their trip, Cole rushed inside to the den and got on his desktop computer. Because of his work with brucellosis, he had a security password to access certain files at the state lab. It was almost midnight when he found the case he knew in his gut was the one to which Norm had referred.

Quentin Ellsworth. He lived on a small spread seven miles out of town off the highway leading to Cora.

Cole knew the Ellsworth name well enough because the rancher had two sons. Both had gone to the same high school as Cole. The one named Silas was Cole's age, a long-distance runner who went to college in Arizona on a track scholarship. The other son, Ezra, was Sally's age. He'd done some bronco riding in the teenage rodeo. Over the years Cole had lost track of both of them.

So it was the cattle on the Ellsworth ranch that had gotten hit with the disease and made Cole believe Mr. Ellsworth could be the culprit wanting revenge. According to the file, one hundred and twenty cows out of the six hundred had to be put down three years ago. Losing that many animals would have set him back a lot financially, especially when the whole herd was under quarantine. The same thing had happened to Cole's father.

His thoughts raced ahead. What if Quentin's anger had been so great, he'd talked his sons into helping him get his revenge? Kept it all in the family. The more he thought about it, the more he had to do some investigating on his own. Why not tonight? Right now would be the perfect time to drive by his ranch and take a look around.

He went to his room for his special goggles. The NVM14 monocular multipurpose system was one of the most adaptable multipurpose night vision devices ever made, and could be used in the daytime while he was searching for elk.

After tucking his tiny notebook and pencil in his shirt pocket, he took off for the Ellsworth ranch. Norm had given them a description of the truck, but Ellsworth could have sold it by now and bought a new one. Like he'd said, they needed proof.

Traffic was light as he drove out of town toward Cora. He used his Garmin GPS to zero in on the ranch in question. He passed a small motel with a truck stop and diner before he came to the ranch turnoff.

Cole made a U-turn and stopped alongside the fencing. He could have driven inside, but chose to take a look through the special goggles. The brown-and-yellow ranch house, probably three or four bedrooms, was on the small side with an addition of a second story on one end. He could see a corral, a barn and a two-horse trailer.

Cole backed up several hundred yards to the end of the fencing, probably marking the end of the man's property. He parked his truck as far off the road as possible, then got out and followed the fencing that enclosed the front area. Lowering his head, he ran along until he was able to see the back of the ranch house.

There he caught sight of a dark blue four-door Toyota. Next to it was a red 2014 Ford one-ton truck, but no sign of the Dodge truck. He zoomed in to get the numbers of both license plates, which he copied in his notebook.

Cole would give the information to Holden who would get the names of the owners and do the research to find out where the Ford truck was purchased. If Ellsworth had turned in his Dodge for a down payment, they'd be a step closer in the investigation.

Having done as much as he could for to-night, he doubled back and took off for home. After he'd taken his shower and got into bed, he saw that Tamsin had texted him while he'd been out prowling around.

You'll be sorry I have your new phone number. Now I'll never leave you alone. Good night, Cole. I love you.

He smiled and sent her a message.

I never want to be left alone, sweetheart. We'll be together tomorrow. I don't know about you, but I can't wait!

Chapter Eight

After an amazingly sound sleep, Cole awakened with a brand-new sense of well-being and stopped in the kitchen for coffee. Louise had made some fresh and he told her how much Tamsin and her mother had loved Doris's gifts. He thanked her, grabbed a piece of toast and took off for town.

The first person he needed to talk to was Holden and he headed for the police station. There was always a lot of activity going on inside. He waited until the desk sergeant told him to go on in to Holden's private office.

The sheriff lifted his head. "What brings you in here first thing?" he asked with a smile.

"I realize Norm couldn't tell us the name of the rancher he's tentatively identified as the arsonist, but I'm sure you know who it is. I wanted to know, too. So I did a little investigating and snooping last night and found the name I was looking for. I'm afraid I did something unethical, if not illegal."

"I guess that's the researcher in you."

"Maybe. Can we talk strictly off the record?"

"What do you think? Pull up a chair."

Cole tore the paper with the license plate numbers out of his notebook and put it in front of Holden. For the next few minutes he explained what he'd done last night after leaving the meeting at the fire station.

"I'm hoping with your resources you can

find out the dealer who sold Quentin Ells-worth the Ford truck I saw parked out in back of his ranch house. Maybe he turned in his Dodge truck for the down payment to get rid of the evidence. It's a long shot, but if so, it could mean he's tried to cover up his tracks."

Holden whistled. "I think you're in the wrong line of business and should join the police force."

"My fiancée would never go for it."

He sat back in the chair. "Fiancée—"

"Yup. On Saturday I drove Tamsin Rayburn to Lander with me to see the rodeo. One thing led to another and I proposed. She accepted, but we're not getting married until I give up firefighting. I told her I'd help until the ar-sonists are caught. If I suddenly suggested that I'm joining the police force instead, she'd never forgive me."

A huge grin broke out on Holden's face. "Congratulations, Cole. She's one beautiful woman and smart. Tamsin audited the books last year. You're a lucky man."

"You have no idea. I guess you've heard our story."

He nodded. "Word gets around. I'm really happy for you, but Chief Powell will have a coronary when you quit. Without your insight, I don't know how long this case would have gone on without any major clues to understanding the problem."

"I never dreamed my career as a biologist would help solve an arson case. But I'm not saying a word to the chief until we've caught this guy."

"I hear you. Let me put these numbers into the database while you tell me more of your theories. You say you remember his sons?"

He nodded. "What if he and his two boys, both in their twenties, have been helping him? Ellsworth might not have gotten any other ranchers involved. Can you find out if they still live at home?"

"Of course. What are their names?"

Cole told him everything he knew. Before long they had feedback on the license plates.

"The blue Toyota belongs to Quentin. The Ford truck is owned by Ezra Ellsworth."

"He's the twenty-five-year-old. Maybe he still lives at home. I wonder about the other son, Silas. And what about Quentin's wife? I wonder if she knows about all those trips he took for gas. If she does drive, where was her car last night?"

Holden eyed him directly. "Thanks to you I've got a lot of investigating to do now. For the time being I'll keep all the information you gave me to myself. Maybe Quentin sold the Dodge truck to Silas. We need to track it down and find out where both sons live."

"Agreed. There's something I'm going to tell you that no one else will know, not even Tamsin. This evening I'm going to switch trucks with Sam. I'm sure you know he's the foreman on my ranch and drives a tan Silverado. Instead of going up in the mountains on my job in the morning, I plan to leave before the sun is up and hang out around the Ellsworth ranch out of sight for three days and nights. That way I can watch the comings and goings without anyone being suspicious."

Holden's gaze narrowed. "Be careful, Cole. This guy plays for keeps."

"Don't worry. I'll pretend I'm a wildlife photographer and stay in one of those rustic little cabins at the Big Horn Motel across the highway. If I see anyone leave, I'll let you know so you can put a tail on them."

"That's a great cover."

"We'll see."

"I'll make sure some patrol cars are right around there. Stay in close touch."

"I'll give you regular updates." He got to his feet. "Let's hope my plan pays off."

TAMSIN RUSHED HOME from the hospital to change into riding clothes. She put on her cowboy hat and hurried outside to Cole's truck, this time with the horse trailer hooked up. Her drop-dead gorgeous cowboy had just gotten out of the cab.

Being engaged to him had changed her whole life. Her feet hardly touched the ground as she ran into his waiting arms. "It feels like a lifetime since last night."

His response was to kiss her harder. Someone driving by let out a loud wolf whistle. Cole only held her tighter. "Are you ready to go bring Flossie to her permanent home?"

"I love the sound of that." She covered his face with kisses before he let her go long enough to climb in the passenger side. After they drove away she turned to him. "I stopped at the office first thing this morning and showed everyone my ring. Heather's going to plan a bridal shower for me. I never thought I'd see this day."

He reached for her hand and intertwined their fingers. "I had a meeting with Holden Granger earlier and told him we're engaged. He told me I was lucky to be marrying such a smart, beautiful woman."

"Even if that's a lie, it's nice to hear."

"Not from Holden. He calls it as he sees it."

Cole drove them to Hilda's and parked along the fencing, out of the way of both cars. "I'll run inside to get our food. Do you want another taco and cola?"

"No. I think I want a hamburger with mustard, pickles and a fresh limeade."

"Got it."

She wondered what made him break out in such a big smile as he walked away from the truck. While she waited for him, she put in the CD from the glove compartment and listened to "Wind River Lovin'." Tamsin loved his music.

When she saw him come back, she turned it off and they ate dinner before starting out again. "My aunt Grace in Afton phoned me at work to congratulate me. She along with Mom and Sally will be planning a shower for us, too. She remembers you from a long time ago when she and Uncle Richard were staying with my folks. She'd been a barrel racer in her late teens and said she could see why

I'd never found another cowboy. You were impossible to match. That's high praise coming from her."

"That's because she loves you. I've been thinking about our wedding, sweetheart."

"So have I. Can we be married at the church where you held your father's funeral? It's where he would have wanted to see you take your vows."

"I was hoping you would say that. It would have been Mother's choice, too."

"Of course."

"But where we have the reception is up to you."

"My parents have already asked if we'll hold it at the house. I know it will mean the world to them. I let them know we won't set the date until the arsonists are caught and you're free from responsibility."

"Good. All I want is your happiness. This

morning Louise told me she and Sam want to host a party for us at their house in Lander."

Tamsin studied his handsome profile. "They love you like a son. I can't imagine anything more wonderful."

As they talked, the Ingram ranch came into view. "We're here."

She nodded. "I let Roy know we were coming to pick up Flossie. Just drive down the road and park in front of the barn. I'll bring her out."

Roy was there to greet them and opened the doors. Tamsin hurried inside and ran over to her mount. "How's my Flossie?" She hugged her neck and tousled her forelock. The horse neighed.

"She's missed you," Roy commented.

"It hasn't been the same without her. We can't thank you enough for letting us keep our horses here. The new barn is going up and it won't be long now before Dad comes for the other horses. We're very grateful."

"You'd do the same for me."

"Anytime."

Tamsin gave her horse a treat, then put on the halter and led her out to the trailer. Cole had opened the door so she could lead her to one of the stalls with a full hay net and water. "We're going to our new home, Flossie. It's not far away. You're going to love it. Cole has half a dozen horses who are going to become your friends."

Cole followed with her gear and saddle. After stowing everything, he came up behind her and put his arms around her waist. "I've been waiting for the day we'd be able to ride together whenever we wanted."

She turned to him. Once again he started kissing her and didn't let her go until she was gasping for breath. Color flushed her cheeks as she walked back outside past Roy and got in the truck. She opened the window to wave at him before they drove off.

It hit her hard that they were going home to Cole's ranch. One day soon it would be *their* home.

Within a half hour she'd walked her around the corral behind the ranch house to let Flossie get used to her new surroundings. Cole brought out her blanket and saddle. Tamsin took over and mounted her while he left her long enough to unhitch the trailer and enter the barn. In a minute he entered the corral on his gelding.

She stared in surprise. "You didn't buy another Arabian."

"Nope. Meet Samson. Strong like his namesake. He's a Missouri Fox Trotter, the most sure-footed animal I've ever ridden in my life when I'm on the trail, let alone in the mountains."

Tamsin led her horse toward his. "Well, hello, Samson. I can tell you're really something. Meet my Flossie." Her roan bay nickered and moved closer. Samson nickered back, causing both her and Cole to laugh. "Don't you have the most gorgeous chestnut coat!"

"Almost the color of your hair," Cole said in an aside that thrilled her. "They're well matched. Let's take them out by the pasture. Samson needs the exercise."

"So does Flossie."

They left the corral side by side. To be in the saddle next to him, knowing this life was going to be forever, caused a wave of excitement to sweep over her. She cast him a sideward glance and discovered he was looking at her. The expression in his eyes told her everything words couldn't. Neither of them could wait until they were married.

By tacit agreement they broke into a gallop that took them out where the cattle were grazing. Cole waved to the stockmen. She slowed her horse. "How many head of cattle do you have?"

"Forty. It's a manageable size for us with so little help."

"We can use my savings to build the herd."

His devastating smile took her breath away. "You want to know how much your future husband is worth?"

"I already have a rough idea." A ranch this size brought in somewhere between eighty and a hundred thousand dollars a year depending on the health of the cattle. "I could buy more land for us. Between my salary and the one you receive from the state, we could build our own little empire."

"That's a compelling thought. I love the way you think. If a baby comes along soon, will you want to keep working?"

"I'm sure I could do it part-time. I guess I never told you I was planning to leave the firm one day and branch out on my own."

"That sounds ambitious."

She frowned. "Too ambitious?"

"If that's how it sounded, you couldn't be more wrong. I'm glad you love your work. Don't you realize how proud I am of you? I'll back you in anything you want to do."

"Sorry I got so sensitive."

"Why did you?"

She let out a sigh. "I guess it's because Lyle asked Sally not to work after they were married."

"What was she doing when he met her?"

"She went to junior college before working

as a secretary at Witcom-Dennison Oil. That's how they met."

"Did she want to keep working?"

"She never said, and I was afraid to ask because it was Lyle's dream to provide for his family. The Witcoms have always had money."

"Well, that's not my dream! I'm going to need all the help I can get."

"I'm so glad you said that!"

"Good. That's one problem we don't ever have to deal with. Race you back to the house, sweetheart."

He took off like a tornado. She tried hard to catch up, but it was impossible. Samson was too fast. By the time she rode into the barn, he was there waiting for her and pulled her off Flossie into his arms.

She came laughing and everything got smothered because he started kissing the daylights out of her. Night had descended by the time they'd put the horses to bed and walked out to his truck.

"I don't want to take you home, but I'm going to have to because I have to leave the ranch at first light. If I take you inside, it's all over and every promise I made to myself and you will go up in smoke."

Once they both got in the truck, she turned to him. "Will you be called out tonight on a fire?" She could hear the anxious throb in her voice.

"No. I always let the chief know when I'm available."

Thank goodness he wasn't going to be doing anything dangerous tonight. "How long will you be gone this time?"

"I'll be back on Friday. I'm planning to take you to a fabulous dinner and dancing. We'll get dressed up and officially celebrate our engagement."

"Ooh. In that case I'm going to shop for a beautiful dress and get my hair done."

"That's fine, but leave it long for me."

"You don't like it when I sweep it up?"

"How can you ask me a question like that? I love you no matter how you wear it. But when you put it up, it only makes me want to pull it down and run my fingers through it."

She laughed all the way back to the apartment.

"Don't worry about Flossie. When you're not there, Sam and Louise will take good care of her. Part of the day they'll walk her out to the corral with the other horses."

At the door to her apartment Tamsin clung to him. "You're too good to me."

He kissed her long and hard. "I only ask one thing of you."

"Anything."

"Stay safe and be here when I get back."

She fought tears. "My greatest wish is that you come home whole and alive for me to love."

"That's a promise."

Tamsin was in agony as she watched him walk back down to his truck and drive away. Even though she knew he loved her and would always come back, she had the horrible premonition that she would always be in agony when he had to leave her. Such was her destiny for loving Cole Hawkins.

WHEN COLE GOT back to the ranch, he found Sam in the kitchen and explained his top secret plans. "Only Holden Granger knows what I'm doing."

"He's a good man. You remember to call me

anytime if you're in trouble. You know where I keep the rifle if you need it."

"Yup. You're the best, Sam."

They hugged before exchanging keys to their trucks. Cole gathered everything he needed and packed up the Silverado before going to bed. Tamsin had left another text message on his phone.

How soon do you want to start a family?

He didn't have to think about it.

Immediately.

Her answer came right back.

Good. That's another problem we won't ever have to deal with. Sweet dreams, Cole.

He smiled.

I guess you know you're the star. Need I say more?

After setting his watch alarm, he climbed into bed, but four thirty in the morning came around sooner than he would have liked. He dressed in Levi's and a cream-colored polo shirt before stealing away from the ranch. With his cowboy hat pulled down low over his forehead, anyone who recognized the truck would assume it was Sam at the wheel.

There were several eighteen-wheelers out on the highway driving both ways. At this hour of the morning, he loved the smell of the sage coming off the hills. In the distance he could see a large group of pronghorn moving swiftly on their limbs. They had a reputation for being the fastest animal in the Western Hemisphere. Tourists came from all over to watch them run.

Another mile and he passed a pack of mule deer crossing the road. Whitebark was renowned for its native animal life that outnumbered the residents ten to one. He loved this world and could never live anywhere else. Thank Heaven Tamsin was a product of it, too.

When he reached the truck stop, it was already busy. He waited behind a semi until it was his turn to load up with gas, taking inventory of every car and rig. With that accomplished, he drove over to the twenty-four-hour diner.

Cole went inside and ordered a full-size breakfast that would hold him for half a day. He sat at the window where he could see the traffic along the highway. At seven thirty he walked over to the motel and checked in for a three-night stay.

The older man handed the credit card back to him. "You here on business?"

"You might say that. I'm a freelance wildlife photographer and am anxious to get some good shots out here in the hills. A few minutes ago a herd of pronghorn raced by. That was a sight any wildlife magazine would pay a lot for. I'm going to watch for them over the next few days."

"They're a sight all right. Stick around this evening and you'll see a family of moose and later on some black bears. They come down to the back of the motel where the tourists wash off after they've gone fishing at the river, hoping for food."

"Can't blame them."

The older man chuckled. "No indeed."

"Thanks for the information. I'll remember to check it out."

He took the key and drove his truck to Cabin

Eight. Once he'd taken his gear inside and locked the truck, he carried his special goggles and a bottle of water in a flight bag and walked out to the highway. The summer traffic was picking up. He crossed over to the other side.

It was a good thing the undeveloped property with clumps of good-size bushes on the other side of the Ellsworth ranch didn't have any buildings he could see. No one would notice him as he retraced his path along the fencing and hid behind one of the largest bushes. From there he had a perfect view of the parking area behind the ranch house. The same vehicles were still there.

Cole sat on the ground and trained his hand-held special goggles on the Ellsworth property. He was looking for movement of any kind. After he'd been holding vigil for an hour, he saw a woman, maybe in her midfifties, come out the back door and get in the blue car. She backed around and drove out to the highway. If he could find out where she was going, that would be a start.

He phoned Holden and gave him a description of the woman and the car. A few minutes later he saw whom he supposed to be Quentin Ellsworth come out and climb into the Ford truck. Cole made another call to Holden as the man backed around and drove out to the highway.

Five hours later nothing had happened. No more movement. Cole hurried back to the motel to freshen up. He waved to the older man who was outside talking to some people. When the way was clear, he grabbed a late lunch at the diner and texted Tamsin.

Wish you were with me. Today the foothills are teeming with pronghorn and white-tailed deer.

He received an instant response.

Am living for the time I can go with you. I hate texting when I'm dying to hear your voice. I'm halfway through hospital audit. Should be done by Friday. If you can, call me when you've set up camp tonight. Stay safe.

That would be easy.

Till tonight. Love you, sweetheart.

Chapter Nine

Instead of going back out there, Cole drove his truck to an area of the truck stop closest to the highway. With his special goggles he could watch for anyone turning toward the Ellsworth property.

At four thirty his vigil paid off when he saw the silver Dodge Ram pass in his line of vision and caught sight of the driver. Silas Ellsworth looked a good fifteen years older than when Cole had last seen him, but his features were unmistakable.

Another twenty minutes and he saw the red truck Ezra drove turn onto the property. Did this mean both sons still lived with their parents, or was this a gathering place while they made plans?

At six, the woman he assumed was Mrs. Ellsworth returned. Cole would wait until dark and then return to the spot behind the bush to see what was going on. This would be the best time to eat dinner and send a text to Tamsin. He had a feeling he wouldn't have time to get in touch with her later tonight, not if he needed to keep a close watch on the Ellsworth ranch part of the night.

Once he'd eaten, he drove his truck back to the motel and would wait until dark to go out again. After Cole came out of the shower, his cell rang and he recognized the caller ID.

"Holden? Any news yet?"

"Yeah. You'll be interested to know that Mrs. Ellsworth is the owner of Lindquist Dry Cleaners in Whitebark. She inherited the business from her family five years ago and reports there on a regular basis."

"So she works outside the home… You wonder how much she knows. That income would have helped their family financially when they went through the brucellosis scare three years ago. Get this—the Dodge truck wasn't sold after all. Silas Ellsworth is driving it and he turned into the Ellsworth ranch at four thirty this afternoon."

Holden whistled. "That means Quentin probably gave it to Silas or else they share it. I've learned that Quentin cosigned on the loan when Ezra bought the Ford truck last winter. Ezra's address is listed as the Ellsworth ranch and he shows no other place of employment.

Interesting that both trucks are duallies that can carry fifty gallons of gas."

"Yup. I'm thinking both sons still live at home and have been helping their father set fires for the last two years. Tonight I'll get the license number off the silver truck and send it to you. If you learn Silas has listed the ranch as his home address, it could mean the boys help their dad with the cattle ranching during the day and carry out all the dirty work at night."

"But we still need proof."

Cole was thinking hard about that. Once the arsonist poured enough accelerant, all he needed were matches rather than an ignition device like a Molotov cocktail. Setting hay on fire whether inside a barn or outside on the property made a conflagration easy because oxygen was plentiful. The hard part was carrying the gas to the area to be burned without being seen.

"Give me a few more days and nights to look inside the truck beds for stashes of gas."

"If only it were that easy."

"I'll figure it out."

"Watch your back, Cole."

"Don't worry. Talk to you soon." They hung up.

Cole had his work cut out and needed to get it done fast. Earlier tonight Tamsin had texted him that she was going to go shopping for a wedding dress while he was away. Their marriage couldn't come soon enough for either of them.

"WHAT DO YOU THINK, Mom?"

Wednesday evening after work, Tamsin had met her mother at Sybil's Bridal Boutique and had tried on three or four dresses. The ivory organza ball gown with the scooped neck and cap sleeves had caught Tamsin's eye and she kept going back to it.

"With the lace overlay on the bodice, it's absolutely beautiful on you, honey."

"I like it the best of the ones I've tried on. I want it to be perfect for Cole."

Her mother rolled her eyes the way Sally did sometimes. "You know what your father says. The wedding is for the bride. The groom is only marking time until it's over."

They both laughed. "Sounds like Dad." She smoothed her hand over the material. "I'll put this dress on hold until tomorrow. After work I'll ask Sally and Heather to come and give their approval."

"I'll tend the baby. She's the sweetest little angel I've ever seen."

"I know. I can't wait to have one just like her."

"First things first," her mother teased, winking at her.

First things first was right! Tamsin was going to have a coronary if there wasn't a wedding night soon.

That evening she texted Cole.

I've found the dress for our wedding. It's on hold until tomorrow. I can't wait to get it. I can't wait for you to come home.

She didn't have to wait long for a response.

Ditto, sweetheart. Be thinking about a honeymoon. Where are you dying to go?

Tamsin wanted him to make the decision.

Someplace neither of us has been.

His answer made her chuckle.

That covers a lot of territory.

She got excited.

How about outside the US? Remember when we used to dream about flying to Australia and swimming in the Great Barrier Reef?

It took him forever to answer.

Shall we discuss a household budget first?

How unromantic of him.

No!

His final answer didn't give her much hope.

Let's talk about it when I get back on Friday. I can hear activity around my camp. Got to run. Love you.

With no more contact from him, Tamsin had to let it go for now. She'd been so full of herself and her plans, she hadn't even asked him how his work was going.

Before she went to bed she made phone calls to Sally and Heather to meet at Sybil's Bridal Boutique at five tomorrow. She wanted their opinion on a veil to go with her gown, too. Tamsin was so excited, she had trouble getting to sleep.

By Tuesday afternoon she'd finished the hospital audit. After saying goodbye to the administrator, she left for the bridal shop. She'd been on a countdown all week. Tomorrow Cole would be back .

Soon after Tamsin got there, Sally arrived. Heather hadn't come yet, so her sister helped her get into the wedding dress she'd picked out. They picked a shoulder-length lace veil that suited her and the dress to perfection.

Sally was all smiles. "No doubt about it. Cole won't be able to take his eyes off you in this."

"That's the idea, but as Mom reminded me, Cole won't care what I'm wearing."

"Too true," Sally agreed. "Lyle was much more concerned what I'd packed for our honeymoon. The less the better."

More laughter ensued. "Did you love the beach?"

"It was great."

"Last night I told Cole I wanted to go to the Great Barrier Reef for our honeymoon."

"How did that go over?"

Tamsin shook her head. "Not well."

"He's a mountain man."

"I know, and I wouldn't change him."

"I know a man who'd give anything to be in his place."

They hadn't discussed Dean until now. "Did Lyle tell him I'm engaged?"

"We both did. It'll take time, but I'm sure he'll get over it. You were wise not to lead him on any longer."

She looked at Sally. "It wasn't wisdom. I just

didn't have strong enough feelings for him. Blame it on Cole."

"Oh, I do!"

Their laughter filled the dressing room before Tamsin's phone rang. She saw the caller ID and picked up. "Heather?"

"I'm sorry, Tamsin. Silas asked me to meet him for an early dinner because he's leaving town tonight and won't be back until Sunday. Will you forgive me?"

"There's nothing to forgive. Sally's here and I'm going to buy the dress. When you can, come over to the apartment one evening soon and I'll model it for you."

"Thanks for being so nice about this."

"Have fun with Silas at dinner. I'll see you at work on Monday."

She hung up and turned to Sally who said, "Is Heather dating Silas Ellsworth by any chance?" Tamsin nodded. "I haven't seen him since he left after high school to go to Arizona on a track scholarship. He was a really fast runner. I wonder what he's doing now?"

"I don't know, but she's seeing a lot of him lately."

"Maybe another wedding is coming up?"

Tamsin smiled. "Maybe." She turned her back to her. "Help me get out of this and I'll take us to dinner before you have to go home."

"*Have* to go being the operative word since I'm nursing Kellie."

"You lucky woman."

"Don't I know it. When will Cole be back?"

"Tomorrow."

"You must be sick of waiting around for him."

"But not for long. Once we're married, we're both going to arrange our schedules around long weekends so I can go with him. At least I'm saying that now. I have to talk to my boss first."

Sally undid the last button on the gown. "That sounds fantastic, but you *can't* go on the fire truck with him."

"Nope. If I tell you a secret, you can't tell a single soul, and that includes Lyle. Please don't promise me if you know you can't keep it."

"I'll have to think about that."

"That's what I thought. Come with me while I take care of the dress."

They left the fitting room and walked up to the front of the store. "Your secret is really that important?"

"Yes."

"Then don't tell me."

"I won't."

"Tamsin—"

AT ONE IN the morning, all was quiet in the back of the Ellsworth ranch house. The lights were out and the two trucks and car had been parked for the night. Cole had been around long enough to know they didn't keep a dog on the premises. A slight cloud cover helped.

It was now or never if he was going to find the gas cans that were necessary to carry out their arson activities.

After lowering his flight bag to the other side of the fence, he climbed over it and took off for the trucks parked in the near distance. At first sight he only saw a couple of bales of hay in each truck bed. There were tool kits along with spades and equipment for repairing fences, but nothing else.

He hid behind the car, but didn't see anything set near the house to draw his interest. The place appeared to be clean of incriminating evidence.

One more look around brought the medium-size barn into view. The barn was the only place he could think of that might hide what he was looking for. Thankful for the cloud cover, he hurried toward it.

Damn. It was locked.

Not everyone locked their barns. That in itself made him suspicious. He walked around the side to a small window and used his special goggles. All he saw was the inside of the tack room. To his frustration, he only spotted gear for the horses. No gas cans.

He moved with care around the end of the barn to the other side. This side contained a larger window. Again he used his goggles. Most of the barn was taken up with horse stalls. He counted four horses. Near the front it looked like farm machinery—maybe a tractor—had been parked, but it was covered with a big tarp. While he considered breaking the window so he could get inside to look around, he heard a noise.

Cole extinguished the light and flattened

himself against the timbered wall. Someone was opening the barn doors. He crept closer to the front of the barn, still staying out of sight. That was when he heard someone start an engine. It sounded like a car or truck engine, not a tractor. He knew the difference.

With stealth, Cole reached in the bag for his goggles and waited until the vehicle emerged from the barn. What he saw was a Ford F-150 in that hospital mint-green color with a US Forest Service logo on both sides of the doors. No doubt it was loaded with gas cans and ready to go, but he couldn't get a fix on the license plate.

Bull's-eye!

He pulled out his phone and called Holden. "I've got news!" Cole told him everything he knew.

"I'm on it, Cole. Great work! Stay in touch."

Within a minute the truck made a stop at

the rear of the ranch house. Two people came outside and got in. Everything Cole had suspected had come true about the Ellsworth family. But what he wanted to know was how they'd gotten hold of a US Forest Service vehicle in the first place.

When the truck disappeared from sight, Cole hurried around to the front of the barn. Silas had left the doors open, no doubt to save trouble when they'd gone on another raid and needed to hide the truck in a big hurry.

Once inside, Cole turned on the flashlight and looked around the area where the tarp had been removed. He spotted a workbench and beyond it a spray-painting machine with several empty cans of various green paint. How old everything was he didn't know, but it was all here. They'd turned the barn into a workshop, maybe as far back as last year when they'd started the first set of fires. He had no idea how they'd manufactured the logo.

But everything made sense. They could drive to the various ranches carrying cans full of gas. No one would suspect a US Forest Service truck being on the off-roads checking for fires and the like in the middle of the night. That was why they'd never been caught!

Cole took pictures of everything with his phone, then shut off the flashlight. Before any more time passed, he ran outside to the fencing and raced toward the highway.

In a few minutes he reached the motel and checked his watch. At two thirty in the morning, somewhere in the county another fire was about to be set. But this time Holden had a lead and before long the police would spot the truck and it would be pulled over.

After packing up, he left the key to the room on the table and took off for Whitebark. En route, he called Holden again, but got his voice mail. Cole left a message about the spray-paint paraphernalia and evidence sitting in the Ellsworth barn. He also sent picture attachments.

Having done everything he could, he headed for the fire station. Not only did he want to help if another report of a fire came in, Cole needed to hear the moment the Ellsworth family were caught red-handed.

The ladder truck was gone when he drove around the back. When he walked inside, Steve, one of the crew looked surprised when he saw him. "I didn't know you were on tonight."

"I'm not. I just got back from my other job."

"It's supposed to be my night off, but I just got a call from the chief. He asked me to come in and help man the skeleton crew who are out in front."

"Is the chief here?"

"Nope."

"That's unusual."

"Agreed. Something must be going on."

"I'll find out from dispatch." He walked through the station to the room where Julia Humphrey was on duty, manning the call center.

She looked up at him and cried out in surprise. "Cole—what are you doing here?"

He frowned. "What do you mean?"

"A call came in twenty minutes ago from someone who said the barn on your ranch was on fire."

His barn?

The horses! Tamsin's horse!

Shocked to the core, he tore out of there to his locker and dressed in his firefighting gear. Then he raced to his truck and drove like a crazy man to his ranch. In the time he'd spent taking pictures and getting back to the motel, the Ellsworths had reached their destination without being stopped and had done their damage to Cole's property.

He broke out in a cold sweat. Was it Sam or Louise who'd called the fire department? The pit in his stomach enlarged. Were they all right?

His body was shaking as he neared the ranch and saw flames billowing in the night air. He could have been looking at the fire on the Rayburn ranch that had been set earlier in the month. Talk about déjà vu.

A huge crowd of neighbors had gathered. He parked along the private road and raced toward the guys working the ladder truck, unable to spot Sam or Louise. The tender truck was around the side. His eyes fused with the captain's.

"How bad is it?"

"There's still one horse inside, but the fire

is becoming fully involved. It's too dangerous to go in there now. The roof's going to cave in any second."

An image of the Ellsworths sneaking onto his property made him wild with fury. "I can't leave it. I'm going in."

"No, Cole—"

But he ignored the captain and ran inside the fast-growing inferno. He could hear the horse screaming in the rear stall. It was Louise's gelding Jimuta and sounded eerily human.

He reached for a rope in the debris that covered the floor and tied it around the Arabian's neck. "Easy, Jimuta. It's Cole. Come on. Let's get you out of here."

Inch by inch he made his way toward the opening, pulling the terrified horse behind him. He imagined this was like being engulfed in a volcanic eruption. A vision of Tamsin swam before him.

Come back whole and alive for me to love.

He remembered those words before a wave of hot air swept down on him. It seemed to burn his lungs before everything went black.

THE PHONE AWAKENED Tamsin at eight on Wednesday morning.

Cole!

She'd arranged to take today off of work so she could be with him after he got home. Without looking at the caller ID, she reached for it on the bedside table, ecstatic because it meant he'd come back to town. She couldn't wait to see him.

"Hello, Cole?" she cried with excitement.

"I'm sorry, Tamsin. This is Louise."

Louise?

Panic gripped Tamsin. She held her phone tighter and slid out of bed. "By the tone in your voice, I can tell something's wrong."

Maybe he was still in the mountains. His truck could have had problems.

"Someone set fire to Cole's barn during the night. Sam called the fire department."

Paralyzed by what she'd just heard, Tamsin sank back down on the side of the bed. "He's been up in the mountains. Does he know?"

"Yes. The firefighters got all the horses out except mine. Cole rushed in to save Jimuta."

"I—I don't understand." Her voice faltered. "Was Cole home?"

"He'd just returned from his trip. When he found out Jimuta was trapped inside, he ran in to save him. As he came out with my horse, part of the roof collapsed and hit Cole on the arm."

Tamsin knew she was going to faint. "You don't mean he's—"

"No, no. He was dragged out and is being

treated for smoke inhalation and some burns on his one arm, but he's going to be fine."

Thank God.

"But you need to come to the hospital as soon as you can because Cole is asking for you."

"I'm on my way. Bless you for letting me know, Louise."

The next hour was a blur while Tamsin dressed and drove to the emergency entrance. Her heart pounded so hard, she had trouble breathing. To make things worse, she had to park at the other end of the visitor parking because so many police cars and fire van units from the county blocked her way to the doors. She noticed vans from two television stations.

"Over here, Tamsin!" She turned her head as Louise came running up and put her arm around her. "He's going to be all right, Tamsin. Sam's with him. I've notified your family. They didn't answer, but I left a message."

"Thank you." In a daze, she followed Louise inside. The emergency room reminded her of a nightmarish war zone in a film. It was noisy, chaotic. A baby was crying. Firefighters were being treated along with other patients. Police had assembled. Tamsin heard one of the staff telling a doctor they had a gunshot wound victim in the trauma center, but all she could think about was Cole.

"You have to check in first." Louise guided her down the hall to one of the rooms where the triage nurse was putting information in the computer. "They're identifying everyone coming into the emergency room."

Tamsin understood, but they had to wait until it was her turn to give her name and phone number. Because arson was a criminal activity, she knew this was a police situation and everyone was being investigated. But she needed to be with Cole and every second away from him was agony.

A few minutes later, an older man who looked like one of the brass Cole often talked about walked in. He nodded to her. "My name is Norm Selkirk. I'm the head of Sublette County Law Enforcement." Cole had talked about him. "If you and Mrs. Speakuna will come in the next room with me, I'd like to ask you a few questions."

It was obvious he'd already talked with Louise. The two of them went with him to the next room down the hall. He invited them to sit down. "Would you tell me your reason for coming to the emergency room, Ms. Rayburn?"

She tried to stay in control. "Cole Hawkins is my fiancé. Mrs. Speakuna phoned and told me that he'd been hurt in the fire set on his own property. He was asking for me, so I came as soon as I could. Please, I need to see him."

"You won't be able to do that for a little while, but don't worry. The doctor is with him."

Don't worry... She had to fight her hysteria. Louise patted her arm.

"Did you know your fiancé's whereabouts before you heard about the fire?"

Why would he ask a question like that? "Yes. He was up in the Winds doing his work tracking the elk. What is this all about? I want to go to him now!" she cried.

"I wish you could, but we're following up an investigation. It won't be long before you're free to see him. For the moment I need to ask you a few questions."

"I don't understand."

"Are you acquainted with Heather Jennings?"

What on earth? "Yes. She and I are both CPAs at the Ostler firm."

"Coworkers, or more?"

"We're close friends."

The man nodded. "Have you met her alleged boyfriend, Silas Ellsworth?"

"No. I mean, I have met him, but not recently." Tamsin was ready to scream.

"Explain what you mean."

"He went to the same high school I did. That was nine years ago. I haven't seen him since."

"Do you know how long she's been dating him?"

She took a deep breath to calm down. "I'm not sure. Maybe for a month. Can I go now?"

"One more question. How well do you trust Ms. Jennings?"

Tamsin jumped to her feet. "I'd trust her with my life. Why are you asking me that?"

"Because she was seen having dinner in

Silas Ellsworth's company a few nights ago. Ms. Jennings would have known about the fire on your father's property through you, Ms. Rayburn. We're trying to ascertain if she was using your association with Mr. Hawkins to gather information on him and learn when he was in or out of town."

Tamsin frowned. "You honestly think she was being my friend to get information?"

"I'm only asking the question."

"For what reason?"

"So she could feed her boyfriend what information Mr. Hawkins had told you since he's been a member of the fire department."

Tamsin was incredulous. "I've never discussed Cole's work with anyone. Furthermore, Heather has never asked. We were close long before she ever met Silas. And why would he be so vitally interested in anything Cole does? I still don't get it."

"He and two others are the alleged suspects in custody at this hour for committing the arson that has plagued the ranchers in this county for two years."

Her heart leaped. She stared at him in disbelief. "They've been caught?" He nodded. "Does Cole know?"

"You'll find out when you're allowed to visit him. Thank you for your time. Wait here and someone will let you know when the doctor says you can see him."

Chapter Ten

Overjoyed by the news that the arsonists had been arrested, Tamsin gave Louise a hug. "It's over."

"Yes. He's been through enough."

"So have you and Sam." *So have I.* Cole had promised that once the case was solved, he'd resign from the fire department and they'd get married.

For the next fifteen minutes they talked about the fire until someone on the staff came in and told them they could see the patient. Tamsin literally ran out of the room with Louise, who led the way to another room farther down the hall and around the corner. The sight of four grubby, foul-smelling firefighters standing around the opening while they laughed warmed her heart.

She heard Cole's voice before peeking inside.

"Get out of here, you guys."

"We're going."

Tamsin recognized Wyatt Fielding, a guy she knew from high school. She also recognized Captain Durrant, who grinned and patted Cole on the shoulder. One by one the other three gave a physical manifestation of their affection and relief by a nudge or some other gesture. Tamsin stayed next to Louise.

She knew Cole had developed deep friendships with his crew back in Colorado. He'd explained that the bond between them was as strong as any blood ties could be. Judging by the behavior of these men here, she could tell how much they cared about Cole already.

This was a part of his life Tamsin had nothing to do with. She knew a moment's feeling of being excluded from a fraternity that could never include her. But it didn't matter. All she cared about was that he'd escaped death from the collapsed roof.

To her overwhelming joy and gratitude, Cole was sitting on the end of the hospital examining table, dressed in jeans and a polo shirt and hooked up to an IV.

The attending physician stood there treating him for smoke inhalation with oxygen. His lower left arm had been bandaged to the wrist. But as far as she could tell, nothing else seemed to be wrong. The man was fearless.

Wyatt made his parting shot. "Try to stay out of trouble for a while, Hawkins!"

"Mr. Hawkins won't be reporting for work for at least a week," the doctor explained. "That burn needs time to heal."

"I'm going to make sure it does!" Tamsin spoke up as she entered the room, because she knew something neither the doctor nor anyone else knew.

"Oh, boy. You're in for it now," Wyatt called out with a gleeful smile. The guys hooted and hollered all the way down the hall.

Her gaze met Cole's. The oxygen mask covered his nose and mouth, but she could tell he was smiling. "You're a sight for these blood-shot eyes," she heard him say. Her heart turned over on itself. "Come closer, sweetheart."

"I'm afraid I'll hurt you."

His deep chuckle thrilled her.

The doctor smiled. "Just make sure he keeps breathing the oxygen. I'll be back in a minute."

Sam left with the doctor, giving her a hug on the way out. Louise followed them, leaving Tamsin alone with Cole at last.

When she ran to her dark blond cowboy, he threw his right arm around her with surprising strength. Worried for him, she eased away enough to cling to his right hand. The tears dripped down her cheeks. "When Louise told me part of the roof collapsed on you, I almost died. You should never have tried to rescue Louise's horse!"

"Jimuta is a special Arabian, named for one of the Arapahoe sun gods and blessed by the chief of their tribe for its remarkable powers. I knew he was frightened, but hoped he would let me get him out because he knew me and my voice."

Tears welled up in her throat. "So many

times you've told me you could never thank Louise enough for taking care of your father near the end. I would say that saving her horse has done more to show your love for her than anything else you could ever do. She was the one who called to let me know you were in the hospital."

"Louise is so modest she would never tell you that Sam risked his life to get the horses out in spite of the flames. I couldn't bear it if anything had happened to them or Flossie. Sam and the stockmen have been taking turns guarding the property at night."

"How did he know about the fire?"

"He'd just come in from his stretch when he thought he heard the horses neighing. He assumed a skunk or a raccoon had gotten in the barn and went out to investigate. That's when he saw the flames and called the fire department."

Tamsin shuddered and gripped his hand harder. "I love them both for their devotion to you and your family. Oh, I wish I could hug you."

"So do I. The doctor says I have to stay in the hospital tonight so they can treat my burn. If everything looks good tomorrow, he'll release me and we can go home where I can hold you in my arms for as long as I want."

Another night of waiting. "Are you in horrible pain from your arm?"

"No. They've given me a painkiller in the IV. My throat is sore, that's all."

"You breathed in too much smoke. I can't believe this happened to you."

"But it's over now and my injury isn't life-threatening. Let's concentrate on our wedding."

She had so much she wanted to talk about, but the doctor came back in followed by the orderlies wheeling a gurney. "We're moving you to the fourth floor." He eyed Tamsin. "If you'll go out to the desk, they'll tell you which room. Give us fifteen minutes."

"Of course. See you soon, my love." She kissed the palm of Cole's hand one more time before hurrying out in the hall where Sam and Louise were waiting. Without hesitation, she hugged them both and broke down weeping for joy that everyone was alive.

AFTER COLE WAS wheeled to the fourth floor along with his IV drip, the nurse helped him into a hospital gown and he was settled in a regular bed. To his relief the doctor had fitted him with an oxygen tube that wasn't as cumbersome as the mask.

While he waited anxiously for Tamsin to come in, knowing this situation was the very reason she wanted him to give up firefighting, he had visitors. The big brass had assembled. Norm, Chief Powell, Commander Rich and Holden walked in and stood around his bed.

Commander Rich cleared his throat. "We know you need rest, but we want to give you a quick update. Because of your heroism for going beyond the call of duty, you'll be getting an award, but it will be given at a later date when your wounds have healed."

"That's not necessary, Commander."

Norm moved closer to the bed. "Every arson victim in Sublette County owes you a debt of gratitude they can never repay."

"Neither can the firefighters," Chief Powell chimed in. "Our courageous men have answered every call to put out those fires. To know the culprits have finally been caught is a gift to all of us. Everyone will sleep better tonight because of you."

A lump had lodged in Cole's throat. "You give me too much credit, gentlemen."

Holden moved over to his other side. "That's not true and you know it. If you hadn't sacrificed yourself to stake out the Ellsworth ranch and discover what was hidden in their barn, we might not have caught up to them for another year, maybe never."

"He's right," Norm muttered. "You could have gotten yourself killed, Cole. They were carrying a rifle. Gunfire was exchanged with Ezra before he was hit and brought in to the hospital. They're treating the gunshot wound to his thigh before he's put behind bars."

"There's more," Holden asserted. "Let's not forget that *you* found the link to the diseased elk and cows that explained the motive for the arson. I'm only sorry we didn't catch the Ellsworths until after they'd set your barn on fire. One of your stockmen told me he saw a forest service truck in the distance, but didn't connect it to the fire. That was all I needed to hear."

"The Ellsworths were very clever," Cole murmured.

"Yup. But one of the guys on patrol spotted the truck returning to their ranch. Once it was pulled over and they exchanged gunfire, the gas cans provided the rest of the evidence. We can all thank God no lives were lost tonight." Holden smiled. "Now we'll get out of your hair. Someone outside is dying to get you to herself."

Cole sighed and lay back against the pillows while the nurse came in to check his vitals and record them in the computer. After she left the room, Tamsin rushed inside looking beautiful in that apple-green summer suit he loved. To his delight she'd left her glossy hair down so it brushed against her shoulders.

"Cole—" She hurried over to the bed and gently caressed the side of his jaw. Her blue eyes traveled over his features. "Can I kiss you?"

"Please." He half groaned the word. She lowered her mouth to give him a tender kiss on the lips beneath the oxygen tube. "I keep thanking God you're alive. Oh, darling—I love you so much."

He cupped the back of her neck with his right hand to give her another one before letting her go.

"Mom and Dad will be here in a few minutes."

"That's good. Now we can set the wedding date. Any time you say."

A troubled look broke out on her gorgeous face. She clung to his hand.

"But you haven't had time to tell Chief Powell you're leaving. Or am I wrong?"

"No. I plan to tomorrow."

She smoothed some tendrils of hair from his forehead. "I was standing outside the door waiting for the men to leave. When they came out, Commander Rich congratulated me for being engaged to a hero who has done a great service for the State of Wyoming."

"He had to say that."

"No, Cole. They all said it. He informed me that he expected me to be at your side when the governor awards you the International Association of Fire Chiefs' Medal of Valor. He said the ceremony would be held next month in Cheyenne for service beyond the call of duty."

"All the firefighters should get one."

Tamsin shook her head. "You never could accept a compliment, but this is one time when you're going to have to!"

"Yes, ma'am."

She kissed his cheek. "After he told me that, Chief Powell shook my hand and said you're a role model for all the men and women who are eager to join the department. He's thrilled you're on the force and hopes you'll be on it for many years to come."

Her eyes teared over. "They're so proud of you. I am, too! After hearing their accolades, I don't know how you're going to tell them that you're leaving the department."

"Tamsin," he whispered, "I gave you my word that we would set the date as soon as the culprits were caught. That day has come."

"But—"

"No buts, sweetheart," he broke in on her. "After tomorrow, this will all be behind us. It'll be a mere formality. No looking back. I wanted to marry you nine years ago and have waited long enough. This is it."

He heard a knock on the door. "That's probably your parents. Tell them to come in."

She walked over and opened it. After hugging her, they moved to the end of his bed while Tamsin came back to his side and grasped his hand.

"What a blessing that you are all right, Cole," her mother said in a tear-filled voice. "Our hearts almost failed us when we heard you were in the hospital. The thought of losing you... You'll never know what we went through."

Moved by her words he said, "Last night was a close call, but today everything's perfect."

"We're so proud of you, Cole."

"We are," Tamsin's father concurred in a solemn voice. "Word that the arsonists plaguing the ranchers in Wyoming for the last two years have finally been caught has gone out over local and national news. They're praising the heroics of one local firefighter from Whitebark named Cole Hawkins who cracked the baffling case for law enforcement."

Tamsin's mother put a hand on his arm. "You're an amazing man, Cole. Tamsin has told us of your sacrifices to help your father years ago when you left to earn a living for the family. If your parents were alive, they'd be ecstatic to tell the world you're their son. We're overjoyed you're engaged to our daughter and feel privileged that one day soon we can call you son."

Overwhelmed by her outpouring of emotion, Cole had to clear his throat. "Thank you. That means a lot," was all he could get out when his heart was so full.

"Whatever we can do for you."

He looked at Tamsin. "We want to plan our wedding, the sooner the better. How about three weeks from tomorrow? Will that give you enough time?"

Tamsin's father chuckled. "My daughter's been ready forever," he teased. "The question is, will you be recovered?"

"I'm fine *now*."

"No you're not!" Tamsin squeezed his hand.

"What about that arm?" her mother asked.

"The doctor says I have a second-degree burn. They're filling me with painkillers and antibiotics to prevent infection. In three weeks I'll be more than fit."

She looked at her husband. "Then I don't see why we can't have a wedding by then. How about Saturday, August 1? But we're going to have to hurry to get the invitations printed and sent out in the next few days. Come on, Howard. We've got things to do. We'll be back tomorrow to see how you are."

"I won't be here," Cole informed her. "The

doctor said he'd release me in the morning. But I'd love you to come to the ranch whenever you can."

"We will, but you mustn't try to do anything for a while."

"Don't worry about that, Mom. I'll be watching him like a hawk," Tamsin said in that determined voice. "So will Louise."

"See you later." As they left the room, the nurse came in carrying a foot-long red fire engine filled with a huge arrangement of red, yellow and orange flowers.

"Oh, Cole—look what you've been sent!"

With a smile, the nurse put the flowers on one of the side tables. "Compliments of the Whitebark Fire Department."

The flowers represented flames. How creative was that? Cole would have burst into laughter if his lungs and throat didn't hurt so much.

"They must love you a lot, Mr. Hawkins. I hear you guys are like brothers." Before she left, she handed him the card so he could read the message.

Did you have to go to so much trouble to get out of work? Don't plan on joining the bull-riding circuit anytime soon, cowboy. We need you back, pronto!

Wyatt had to have been the one responsible for all this. Cole had to admit the camaraderie with the crew was something he was going to miss. They went through a lot together every time they had to go on a run. Nothing got the adrenaline surging like the beeper going off. You never knew what was waiting for you, but one thing was always certain: the guys had your back.

Much as Cole loved his work in the mountains, he'd learned to love firefighting when he'd first started out in Colorado. In his gut, he knew it would always stay with him. While he contemplated the step that would take him away from that career, exhaustion took over. He fought to stay awake for Tamsin's sake, but it was a losing battle.

TAMSIN STAYED AT Cole's side while he slept and studied the card for a long time. *We need you back, pronto.*

She'd seen the expression in his brown eyes earlier and would never forget the look of loss and regret registered there. Right then his thoughts had been far away from her and she knew why.

The nurse had spoken the truth. They *were* like brothers. Tamsin had felt it while she'd been outside the emergency room cubicle earlier listening to their banter. Cole had promised to give up firefighting so she would marry him. But she couldn't shake off the feeling that he would be giving up something so important to him, it might affect him in ways she hadn't considered.

Tamsin stayed with him until evening. The nurse took out the IV and they ate dinner together. He was given soft foods he could tolerate. She knew his throat was sore. Tamsin didn't encourage him to talk. Instead she turned on the TV to watch the news. Cole featured prominently, but the names of the arsonists hadn't been released yet.

"I can't believe that the Ellsworths were the ones responsible. They were both really nice guys in high school." Her body quaked. "I'm still trying to digest the fact that Ezra got shot trying to kill a state trooper."

"Their father lost too many cows to the disease and none of them could get over it."

"You wonder if his wife knew."

"Probably."

"How awful."

"First-degree aggravated arson means they'll all do time in prison."

She moaned. "Commander Rich interrogated me this morning." Cole looked at her with a startled expression. "He was trying to find out if my friend Heather was involved in any way because she's been dating Silas. The idea was absurd, but it's so sad. I can tell she really likes him. Now I know why she couldn't meet me at the bridal shop on Thursday."

"What happened?"

"She said Silas was leaving town and wanted to have an early dinner with her. To think he was planning to burn your barn before the night was over. I can't comprehend it that they have set so many fires with no remorse."

"Including your father's barn."

Tamsin nodded. That was a night she'd never

forget, but that was because Cole had come home and the shock of seeing him again had brought her so close to a faint, she'd slumped against Dean.

"Poor Heather's going to be devastated when the police release their names to the press."

Cole sounded resigned when he said, "It wouldn't do any good to ask you not to think about it, so I won't. Your fears for me really came to fruition, didn't they, sweetheart? But no more on that score from now on."

Somehow that didn't make her happy. Not at all. She turned off the news and got up to kiss his lips. "You're exhausted. I'm going to leave for the apartment so you can get your rest. We'll text all night if you want. I'll be here first thing in the morning and drive you home when it's time."

"I don't want you to go."

"Yes, you do. You just don't want to hurt

my feelings. It's because that's the way you're made. But when the doctor came on rounds, he checked your burn, put on a fresh dressing and told you to get a lot of sleep. I heard him say he's keeping you on oxygen until morning. That means it's time for me to leave. Good night, my love. Sweet dreams."

"One more kiss."

Against her better judgment she pressed a quick one to his lips and hurried out of the hospital room. She drove home exhausted and eager for a shower. When she was ready for bed, she phoned Sally and they talked for at least an hour about everything, including the Medal of Valor Cole was going to receive.

"Your husband-to-be has become a celebrity in every sense of the word. The news said he cracked the case. How did he do it exactly?"

"I don't know yet. All that smoke bothered his throat. Maybe tomorrow it'll feel better and he'll be able to tell me what happened behind the scenes. Mr. Selkirk praised him to the skies. That lets me know there's a lot Cole hasn't told me."

"He's a dark horse, that one."

"If you want to know the truth, Cole is so impossibly honorable at times, it's scary."

"That's an odd thing to say."

"Not if you knew what I know."

"What *do* you know?"

"A lot. There is one thing I could tell you, but it would be for your ears only. No sharing with your husband."

"You're kidding—"

"I knew it! You can't keep anything from him, so I'll say good-night."

"Tamsin—tell me. I swear I'll never repeat it."

"Then I'll trust you. When I told Cole I couldn't marry a firefighter, he said he would give it up because he didn't want to lose me. He promised that once the arson case was solved, he would turn in his badge. That's why we've set the date for three weeks from Saturday." A lump lodged in her throat. "That's the kind of honorable I'm talking about."

For once, silence reigned on the other end. "Sally? Are you there?"

"Yes," she answered in a quiet voice.

"What's wrong?"

"I was just thinking how hard it might be for Cole to give up firefighting, but Lyle is just coming in," she whispered. "I'll have to talk to you tomorrow. Bye for now."

The line went dead.

Tamsin hung up, then sent Cole a text telling him she loved him. Afterward she went to bed. He'd probably gone to sleep and that was why he didn't respond.

For most of the night she tossed and turned,

troubled by her own thoughts and her sister's comment about Cole giving up firefighting. At five in the morning, she sat up in bed with a gasp, recognizing what was wrong. Her unrest had started at the hospital when she'd heard the fire crew joshing with Cole in the emergency room. The strange feeling attacking her had never left.

Instead it had grown much worse until she realized she had to do something about it. Sally's silence had only put the punctuation point on it. Armed with a plan, Tamsin got up and took time to do her nails and curl her hair. She wanted Cole to take one look at her and fall in love with her all over again.

After going to her closet, she found the summery dress she was looking for. It was a blue-and-white print with short sleeves and a scooped neck. She chose white high-heeled sandals to go with her outfit.

For a final touch she wore the adorable little enamel bluebell-shaped earrings he'd given her in high school for Christmas. They'd stayed in her jewelry box all these years, her one keepsake from him she could never part with. Thankful that she hadn't, she went in front of the bathroom mirror to put them on. They matched the color in her dress to perfection. Would he even remember them?

By eight o'clock she was ready and drove to the hospital. She was so excited to see Cole, she was feverish. After reaching the fourth floor, she hurried down the hall to his room. She noticed the orderlies delivering breakfast trays. Her beloved was probably still on soft foods.

But when she reached his door there was a sign that said Do Not Disturb. Nervous that something was wrong, Tamsin rushed down the desk to inquire about him. The charge nurse looked up.

"The doctor should have taken the sign down after his rounds. You can go in."

Relief washed over Tamsin. She raced back to his door. When she walked in, she found him sitting up in his bed watching the news. The oxygen tube had been removed and he looked wonderfully normal to her. Their eyes fused before he turned off the TV.

"I thought you'd never get here." His voice sounded stronger.

"I was afraid to come any sooner and disturb you."

"You can always disturb me. Come here."

She ran around to his right side. He reached for her with his free arm. Once their mouths met, they kissed long and passionately.

Tamsin heard him moan. He finally took a breath. "You smell and look divine. That must be a new dress. What are you trying to do, give me a heart attack?" He smoothed a tendril behind her ear and she heard him draw in his breath.

"You're wearing the bluebell earrings I gave you. I didn't know you kept them. They're the color of your eyes."

"Your gift made my Christmas. I could never part with them. Don't you know I loved you to death even then?" She kissed him harder. "The nurse told me the doctor has already been to see you. How's the burn?"

"Good. He has released me to your care and I've eaten breakfast. Are you ready to take me home?"

"I think you know the answer to that question."

"Yeah. I do. I'll ring the nurse."

Within a few minutes one of the orderlies appeared with a wheelchair for Cole. The nurse handed him a bag that held his belongings and some medication from the pharmacy. Tamsin reached for the flower arrangement. "I'll carry this down."

"We'll save the engine for our first boy to play with."

She laughed. "Girls like fire engines, too."

His smile disappeared as he stared at her. "Not all girls."

With those piercing words, her excitement faded because she was the person responsible for producing that remark from him.

She tried not to show it, but by the time they got settled in her truck with the flowers put in the back seat on the floor, Tamsin knew it was time to have the most important talk of their lives. The muggy hot morning portending rain later on seemed to close in on her. Until she said what was on her mind, nothing would be right.

After they started through town, she couldn't hold her feelings back any longer. "Cole—there's something I have to say to you."

Because of the wound on his left arm, he didn't try to touch her as they drove. "It must be serious. You look like you've just lost your best friend. Where has the most gorgeous woman on the planet suddenly disappeared to?"

She had trouble breathing. "That woman needs to ask your forgiveness for something unforgiveable she's done."

He smiled, trying to lighten the mood. "You've never done anything that's unforgiveable."

"That's not true. We both know I have." Her hands clung to the steering wheel as she drove toward his ranch.

"Sweetheart—tell me what's wrong. As long

as you're not going to remove the ring I gave you, I can handle anything."

By the time they reached the parking area of his property, she was a nervous wreck. "Maybe you'd better stop the truck before we have an accident."

Chapter Eleven

Tamsin came to a halt with a jerk, almost skidding into his truck. She managed to shut off the engine before burying her face in her hands. "I should never have asked you to give up your career as a firefighter. It was wrong of me. Selfish. I was only thinking of my own wants and needs, never once considering what I was asking of you. I've been so unfair to you."

By now the tears were gushing down her cheeks. "I'm ashamed of how I've acted and what I've put you through." She lifted her head to look at him. "When the flowers came and I saw that look in your eyes after you read the card from the crew, I could see what the cost would be for you to give it up. I knew then it was the last thing you wanted to do.

"Cole—for you to turn your back on something you love so much in order to marry me would kill me. I couldn't bear to be the reason you go through life feeling robbed of something so important to you. What I'm trying to say is that I don't want you to give up firefighting. I *won't* let you do it!"

His features suddenly hardened into an expressionless mask. "I'm afraid it's too late for that. Before you arrived at the hospital this morning, Chief Powell phoned to check up on me. That's when I told him I was resigning and why. The deed is done."

"No—" Her horrified cry rang out in the cab.

"No?" By now his face had lost color. "Less than a month ago, I recall you telling me you couldn't marry a firefighter, not under any circumstances. Since marriage to you was more important to me than anything else, I made the decision to get out.

"Now that I've honored my commitment to you and followed through on my part, I'm hearing something else. I don't seem to be getting this right no matter what I do. Why don't you just tell me the truth, Tamsin Rayburn? What you're trying to say is that a marriage between us isn't going to happen under any circumstances. Maybe you're more hung up on Dean Witcom than you realized."

"Cole—"

But he ignored her and got out of the truck. Grabbing the bag from the back seat, he started walking toward the front porch of the ranch house.

"*Wait—your flowers*—I'm coming in with you so we can really talk!"

He wheeled around with a wintry expression. "But I'm finished *really* listening to you. Keep the flowers and the ring. When I wrote 'Doomed to Love Her,' it turns out I was a prophet after all."

The air left her lungs as she watched him disappear inside the house. He hadn't given her the chance to express everything that was in her heart. Right now she saw no way of reasoning with him. There was only one thing she could think to do. Taking her courage in her hands, she backed around and headed for town.

When she neared the fire station, she found a parking place along the street and got out. With no ladder truck in sight, she imagined they were out on another call. Thank Heaven it wasn't the arsonists this time!

Tamsin hurried inside and approached the man at the desk. The sign said Sergeant Perez. He looked up at her, but she didn't recognize him. "May I help you?"

"I hope so. Would it be possible to speak to Chief Powell?"

"I'm afraid he's in a meeting."

She bit her lip, fearing that he was already telling the higher-ups about Cole's resignation. "Do you have any idea how long it will last?"

"Sorry."

"Do you mind if I wait?"

"What's your name?"

"Tamsin Rayburn. This is of life and death importance." She wasn't lying about that.

"Just a moment."

He left his desk and walked down the hall. A few minutes later he returned with Chief Powell.

"Ms. Rayburn. I understand you wanted to see me."

"If I could. You have no idea how badly I need to talk to you."

"Then come with me."

"Thank you."

She followed him down the hall to his office. He walked behind his desk and indicated she should take a chair.

"I'm surprised to see you here. I thought you'd be with your fiancé. He was supposed to go home from the hospital this morning, wasn't he?"

"Yes. Actually I just drove him to his ranch. But something came up on the way. Something awful, and only you can fix it." She stared at him through her tears. "Please tell me you'll help me."

"If I can."

"Cole told me he talked to you earlier this morning and turned in his resignation."

"That's true."

Her heart sank. "Did he tell you why?"

"He said it was for personal issues, but he didn't go into specifics." That sounded like Cole. Honorable to the end. "For a man who's as suited for this kind of work as he is, Cole must have had a very strong reason."

"He did," she said softly. "A month ago I told him I couldn't handle being married to a firefighter and I turned down his proposal," she stammered. "You see, nine years ago there was a terrible fire in the Bridger Wilderness and my best friend's father was burned to death along with some other firefighters."

"I remember," he murmured.

"It was so awful. When I saw the pain his family went through, I knew then I could never be married to one and told Cole how I felt."

"Ah."

"He came back at me with a compromise and said he'd give it up, but not until the arsonists were caught. Once they were identified and brought down, he'd quit the department and we'd get married."

She wiped the moisture from her cheeks. "I was out of my mind at the time and agreed to that compromise so we could be married. I loved him so much and have waited so long for him to come home from Colorado, I wasn't thinking about what he'd be giving up to marry me.

"But I know now that Cole will never be really happy again if he can't do what he loves. He's the most amazing guy. I've never known a man so outstanding at everything he does. He plays guitar, composes music, and was one of the top bull riders on the circuit. You name it, Cole can do anything. When gifts were handed out, he got most of them. Sometimes I think he's too good to be true." Her voice wobbled.

The chief nodded with a smile. "I agree. Has he told you how he cracked the case?"

"No. His throat hurt too much and I didn't want him to talk. But he'd never tell me anyway because he's too modest."

"Then let *me* tell you."

Tamsin sat there in amazement while she learned where Cole had really been the night he said he was heading to the mountains.

"He'd figured out through his work as a biologist that Quentin Ellsworth had been the rancher to lose a lot of calves to brucellosis. Cole put two and two together and knew Ellsworth had a strong motive for committing arson."

"Just like he figured out why some of the ranchers were being targeted."

"Exactly. On the night in question, he stayed at a motel across from the Ellsworth ranch, and sneaked into their barn where he discovered a truck they'd painted up to look like it belonged to the US Forest Service. When they left to go light a fire on Cole's property, they rode in that truck so no one would be suspicious."

She shook her head. "It's a miracle they didn't shoot him."

"Cole was too careful. He took pictures and sent us the information about the spray-paint machine. He took the Ellsworths on single-handedly and risked his life to get the news to the sheriff. Without his smarts, we might never have found out who was lighting those fires. The last thing we want is for him to leave the department."

Tamsin leaned forward with her hands clasped. "Then will you call him and tell him that you won't accept his resignation? I want him to stay on so he'll be happy, but he won't listen to me."

"You're a very wise woman who knows there's nothing worse than a firefighter who doesn't have the support of his wife. So I'll tell you what I'm going to do. We'll both drive out to his ranch right now and I'll reinstate him."

She jumped to her feet. "You mean it?"

He smiled. "It will be my pleasure. I've learned a little wisdom in my older age. A fire-fighter with a bad heartache is no good at all. Cole came back to Whitebark for you. Let's put him out of his misery once and for all, shall we?"

Tamsin loved him so much for saying that, she ran over and hugged him.

"COLE?" LOUISE'S VOICE. Since taking a shower and changing into clean jeans and a T-shirt, he'd been working on the computer.

"What is it?"

"I know you wanted to be left alone, but you've got company."

"I'm trying to catch up on data I need to send into the lab."

"Shall I tell Chief Powell that?"

His head jerked back. "*He's* here?"

"Yes."

Why the devil had he come over? "I'll be right out."

He left the den and walked out to the living room, but stopped dead in his tracks. In his line of vision he saw Tamsin, the chief and the flowers placed on the coffee table in that order.

"Chief Powell?"

"You look good for someone just released from the hospital. Since our talk on the phone this morning, I had a visit from your fiancée."

Tamsin stood next to the chief. In that stunning blue-and-white dress, her beauty only exacerbated his anger that she'd dared to come near him.

"What's going on?"

"I'm here to tell you that I won't be accepting your resignation under any circumstances. I didn't know all the facts when we spoke earlier, but Ms. Rayburn has filled in the blanks to my complete satisfaction."

Cole shook his head in shock.

"When you get back from your honeymoon, let me know when you're ready to report for duty. By then you'll be a husband. We'll work out a schedule that will be compatible with your elk research activities and still give you time to enjoy this wonderful woman you're about to marry. After what she revealed to me, she gets what you're all about. They don't come any finer."

He felt his heart start to pump blood again. His gaze shot to hers.

"Get well now and take care of that burn. The next time I see you will be at the wedding. The crew can't wait, but they'll have to come in shifts."

After the chief left the house, Tamsin walked toward Cole. "If you hadn't gotten out of the truck so fast, I would have told you that I won't marry you if you don't stay with the department. You survived the fire the other night. That gives me faith that you'll do it again and again. I love you, Cole. Your happiness is all that matters to me."

Bursting with emotions he couldn't contain, Cole reached for her and pulled her into his arms, being careful with his left. He kissed every inch of her face. "If you hadn't come back…"

Three weeks later

THE DESK CLERK checked his computer. "Mr. Hawkins? Welcome to Kauai." He handed Cole the card key. "We hope you and your wife enjoy your stay while you're in Hawaii. If you'll follow the porter, he'll carry your luggage and show you to your condo. It's right on the beach as you requested."

Now that Cole's left arm had healed to a great extent, it was wonderful to put it around Tamsin's shoulders without wincing. They left the lobby and followed the path around flowering gardens and grassy grounds to their honeymoon suite.

The gentle surf in Poipu, plus the swaying palms, had a magic feel this time of night. Tamsin clung to him. "Everything looks so perfect, it's like walking into a picture postcard. But that's because I'm with you and I'm afraid I'm dreaming that we're actually here."

The porter opened the door of their bungalow and set their bags down in the little sitting room. Cole gave him a tip and the man left.

Tamsin wandered over to the window where the breeze came through off the ocean. "I love this temperature." She turned to him. "Isn't this paradise?"

"The air is like velvet." He walked over and cupped her face. "I'm sorry it's not the Great Barrier Reef, but we didn't have time to get passports."

"It doesn't matter. We can go there someday. As far as I'm concerned, we had the perfect wedding. My parents love you, Cole. Everyone does. To be honest, I'm happy to get you away from the crew and be alone with you at last. I don't want to share you with anyone, and I think Kauai could easily be the Garden of Eden."

"Lucky Adam if Eve looked like you."

She kissed his lips. "If you want to know the truth, I feel sorry for Eve. Adam could never measure up to you."

"How do you know?"

"Because she'd never seen him master a bull or muster cattle on his horse. She never knew what it was like to hear him play his guitar and compose songs to her."

"I'm sure he did many things that impressed her. Don't forget. All they had was each other, which meant they had to be creative. That's the part I like best." He began kissing her, knowing he never had to stop.

"When I walked down the aisle with Daddy and saw you standing at the altar in your tux, my legs almost gave away. It was a good thing I had him to hold on to."

"That was pretty exciting all right. Sam asked me if I was okay. He knew my heart was pounding out of control, like it is right now. Will you make love to me, Tamsin?"

"You don't have to ask me that. I was ready the night we got engaged. You were the one who said we had to wait."

"Are you sorry?" He picked her up and carried her into the bedroom.

"I don't know. I'm a little scared. Maybe this is how Eve felt the first time. If she was like me, she wanted to be all things to the spectacular, incredible man she'd married. What if she couldn't measure up to his expectations?"

"Men have the same fears, sweetheart."

"Not you. You're not afraid of anything."

"Only once was I truly afraid. It was the night of the fire on your property. I found out one of the Rayburn girls was married. That's the night I came close to losing it, until Wyatt told me it wasn't you. Now you're married to me and I don't want to talk anymore."

IN THE EARLY morning hours, Tamsin awakened, hungry to know her lover's possession again even though they'd made love throughout the night. Cole had taken her to heights she'd never even dreamed about. It was a revelation to her. He made her feel immortal. She wanted to know that feeling over and over again.

Though he was sleeping, she started kissing his throat and inched closer to his lips, willing him to wake up enough to thrill her once more. Tamsin knew she was being shameless, but she couldn't help it. He'd awakened the passion in her. She was on fire for him. Unable to handle it any longer, she covered his mouth with her own.

Before long she felt his powerful legs stir.

Soon he was running his fingers through her hair and then it was Cole rolling over to trap her body. "I know I've died and gone to Heaven," he spoke against her lips.

Heaven was right. Four hours later they both awakened with her head lying against his shoulder, a possessive arm around her hips. They looked into each other's eyes.

"Good morning, Mrs. Hawkins. How do you feel?"

She smiled. "You know exactly how I feel, Mr. Hawkins. I've never been so happy in my life, so…complete."

"That's the perfect word, my love."

"To think we had to wait nine long, agonizing years to know this kind of bliss." Suddenly the tears welled up inside her and she couldn't stop them from running out of her eyes. "I know I shouldn't think about it, but after making love with you all night, it's hard not to resent all the time we lost, all the pain we had to endure."

He kissed her mouth quiet. "Why don't we make a pact and never look back. Today is the start of our new life together. Let's make up for lost time and fill it."

"I want that, too, Cole. I'm sorry for bringing it up."

"Stop apologizing to me. I'll order breakfast and then we'll plan our day."

She traced his lips with her finger. "I know what I want to do."

"So do I." He half growled the words.

Though they'd flown all this way to Hawaii, they only left their bungalow to go out for a swim in the ocean. Then they came back to their haven, never seeming to get enough of each other. Maybe it was because they'd had to wait so long to be together, they weren't that eager to do anything but just express their love. Maybe it was the fear that their happiness could be snatched away.

All she knew was that when it came time to fly back to Wyoming, Tamsin wasn't sorry. She couldn't wait to live with Cole and make the ranch house their own home. It had been a dream of hers for such a long time.

After Sam and Louise picked them up at the airport in Jackson Hole, they drove straight to Lander for the barbecue they'd planned for the newlyweds. Many of their friends from the tribe had gathered behind Doris and Riley's house.

The warm August night couldn't have been more perfect. Cole pulled her down on the grass with him while they watched the grass dance and the hoop dance accompanied by drums, rattles and bells.

Tamsin loved the grass dance performed

by the men. They wore tassels of grass that swayed with their movements, imitating the wind whistling through the grass on the plains. The hoop dances were creative versions of the animals of the plains. The night seemed enchanted, especially when Cole kept kissing her at every opportunity.

The tepee stood tall against the sky, symbolic of the great Arapahoe nation that was here before the white man. Though Tamsin had loved being in Hawaii, she'd never known a more romantic night than this one with Sam and Louise's family and people.

They celebrated until far into the night. When Cole finally helped her to her feet, Tamsin's heart pounded hard as he led her to the tepee for the night. She could easily pretend she was an Indian maiden following her warrior lover to his tepee.

Knowing what awaited her during the night, she could hardly contain her excitement. Cole lit the lantern and spread out the double sleeping bag.

"Sweetheart? Tonight we're going to do it the Arapahoe way."

"What do you mean?"

"Don't wear anything to bed." He removed his clothes and got under the covers. "Now it's your turn." He was still sitting up. She hesitated for a moment. "Surely you're not shy around me after what we experienced on Kauai."

"Is this really the custom?"

He let out a deep laugh that filled the tepee. "I have no idea. I haven't asked Sam."

"Oh, you!"

She disrobed with maidenly modesty and slid under the covers next to him.

To her surprise he pulled something out from under the covers. It looked like a roll of wrapping paper, probably two and a half to three feet in length. He handed it to her.

"What's this, darling?"

"Open it and find out."

Her hands fairly shook as she took off the paper, hoping not to tear anything. In a minute the whole paper came off to reveal a wrapped-up skin. Cole helped her open it all the way.

A gasp fell from Tamsin's lips when she realized what it was.

Everything an Indian does is in a circle, and that is because the power of the world always works in circles, and everything tries to be round. The sky is round and I have heard the earth is round like a ball, and so are all the stars. The wind in its greatest power whirls, birds make their nest in circles, for theirs is the same religion as ours. The sun comes forth and

goes down again in a circle. The moon does the same and both are round. Our tepees were round like the nests of birds. And they were always set in a circle, the nation's hoop. Even the seasons form a great circle in their changing, and always come back again to where they were.
—Chief Black Elk

"Doris made this painting for us!"

He nodded. "She likes you very much, or she wouldn't have gone to this kind of trouble and used an elk skin. It's a great honor, Tamsin."

"I know it is. We'll put it wherever you think it should go in our home."

"Our home." His brown eyes shone with a luster she'd never seen before. He moved the skin away from their bag and put out the light.

"Come here, sweetheart. I want to relish this night with you in my arms."

Tamsin nestled against him. "It feels so surreal to be in this tepee sleeping out under the stars. Everything seems so right. Sam and Louise are wonderful people with such a rich heritage. I'm grateful to be able to share it."

"That's how I feel about you. Blessed beyond belief to realize you're my wife."

She kissed him with longing. "We're going to have the most wonderful life. I can't wait until we have a baby."

"I think we've done a pretty good job of working on it so far. But until our first one arrives, let's just savor the two of us having this time together. You have no idea how jealous the guys are who aren't married yet. I hate to tell them they'll never find a woman like you."

"Like I said, I feel sorry for Eve, but I guess

it's true that what you *don't* know can't torture you."

More laughter rumbled out of Cole before he reached for her and taught her a new meaning for the word *ecstasy*.

Chapter Twelve

"Sally?"

Tamsin ran through Sally and Lyle's new home at noon and found her in the nursery.

"Shh." Her sister turned to her. Tamsin looked in the crib. Their precious four-month-old, Kellie, was asleep, curled up in one corner clutching her blanket.

"Sorry." She mouthed the words. They walked out and down the hall to the front room.

Sally smiled at her. "What went on in the

376 **The Right Cowboy**

mountains to make you look and sound this excited?"

"It's what happened when we got back this morning. I just came from seeing your OB. We're expecting!"

The two sisters hugged each other in happiness. "Does Cole know?"

"Not yet. I came here first."

She cocked her head. "Don't you think he'd want to know first?"

"Yes, but because you suspected I was pregnant last week before we left on our last trip, I decided to tell you first. You've always had an uncanny knack for knowing what was going on with me. Have I told you how much I love you for seeing into my heart and urging me to be honest with Cole? I'm so happy every minute of my life with him, I'll be forever indebted to you."

Sally shook her head. "Even if you made it

hard for him, he wouldn't have given up. You two were meant to be together."

"I know we are." But her smile faded. "Tell me one thing. How's Dean been since he moved to Riverton?"

"Believe it or not, Lyle says he's met someone."

Tamsin's heart clapped for joy. "Oh, I hope it's the real thing for him. I'll always love him in my own way."

"I think he knew that. I love him, too. It would be great if this was the real thing." She grabbed Tamsin's hand and pulled her over to the couch. "I want to hear details about the baby."

"I'm six weeks pregnant."

"Knowing you, you've got names picked out already."

"If it's a boy, I want to name him after Cole's father. He worshipped that man."

"And if it's a girl?"

"Cole will probably have his own ideas on that."

"What do you bet he writes a dozen songs about him or her before the baby's born."

Tamsin nodded. "Would you and Lyle come to the ranch for a surprise dinner tonight and bring Kellie? I've already invited Mom and Dad. Sam and Louise will be there as well as Doris and her husband. We'll have a big family celebration. I'm going to make a cake that says 'Proud Papa.'"

"Cole will die."

"That's the plan, figuratively speaking. I swear, Sally. If anything ever happened to him..."

"Hey—I thought you were over thinking like that. You're going to be a mother. Concentrate on the family you've started. Another Hawkins is on the way. It'll either be a barrel racer or a bull rider. Frankly, I hope it's a girl for Kellie to play with. Have you seen the little tiny baby cowboy boots at the shop in town? They're so cute!"

"What's so cute?"

Lyle had just walked into the living room.

"Oh, honey—Tamsin has the best news on earth!"

"I already knew that."

"How do you know?" Tamsin asked.

"My wife told me last week. Congratulations." He walked over and hugged her.

The three of them broke down laughing and suddenly they could hear the baby crying.

Lyle headed out of the room. "You two go on plotting while I get her. You and Cole have no idea what you're in for now."

Tamsin couldn't wait. She jumped up from the couch. "I've got to go home and get ready for Cole. Tell Lyle goodbye for me. See you tonight."

She raced out of the house to her truck, unable to get home fast enough. A bright new future awaited them. He just didn't know it yet.

* * * * *

LET'S TALK

Romance

For exclusive extracts, competitions and special offers, find us online:

f facebook.com/millsandboon

⊙ @millsandboonuk

🐦 @millsandboon

Or get in touch on 0844 844 1351*

For all the latest titles coming soon, visit millsandboon.co.uk/nextmonth